On Baker Street

Julia Lane

Order this book online at www.trafford.com
or email orders@trafford.com

Most Trafford titles are also available at major online book retailers.

Printed in the United States of America.

ISBN: 978-1-4269-7302-4 (sc)
ISBN: 978-1-4269-7303-1 (hc)
ISBN: 978-1-4269-7304-8 (e)

Library of Congress Control Number: 2011912349

Trafford rev. 07/18/2011

 www.trafford.com

North America & international
toll-free: 1 888 232 4444 (USA & Canada)
phone: 250 383 6864 ♦ fax: 812 355 4082

This book is a work of fiction. Any references to historical events, real people, or real locales are used fictitiously. Other names, characters, places, and incidents are products of the author's imagination, and any resemblance to actual events or locales or persons, living or dead, is entirely coincidental.

To God for giving me a dream and Robin Meade, whose book is an inspiration for me. Thank you for writing it.

INTRODUCTION

This story is about five families who lived in Greensboro, North Carolina, on Baker Street in the projects called the Hamptons. They faced trials, triumphs, heartbreak, betrayal, suicide, adultery, and murder. Their dreams were their survivors. They all had one thing in common—a mission to get out, no matter what that took. One lived in the projects based on financial status. Everyone who lived there had some sort of financial hardship or mental or physical disability. Single parents and divorcées called the projects home.

No one chose to live in the Hamptons. Living in the projects was a choice that unfortunate circumstances forced on you—circumstances that could happen to anyone at any unexpected time.

This story is about the parents and these five families and the unfortunate luck that landed them in the Hamptons. It's about their dreams, hopes, and prayers for their offspring—their dreams that their children would grow up with the determination and will to get out. This story will tell you about the families' past, present, and future. We will begin with each family's past and the circumstances leading up to their arrival in the Hamptons.

The Hamptons was the worst of all the projects. Drugs, loud music, drive-bys, fights, break-ins, gangs, and rape were the norm. No mailperson, or any delivery person for that matter, would deliver there. No neighborhood watch existed. The residents were afraid to get involved. Even the police took their time when answering a 9-1-1 call.

This neighborhood was about to experience an unexpected change that would forever affect the lives of the people in the Hamptons.

Part I

THE PAST

Chapter One

JACKIE AND FAMILY

Jackie's was the first family to move onto Baker Street. Jackie moved to the neighborhood with her two young sons, Jamal and his younger brother, Travis. They instantly became popular. Jackie had a sexy appeal about her. People compared her legs to Tina Turner's. No one believed kids had come out of that body of hers. She looked younger than her age. When the kids were born, she'd become a stay-at-home mom, but she'd been a very active one. It had been her husband, Travis Sr.'s, decision that he would take care of all the family's financial needs, while Jackie took care of the household and the kids.

Travis Sr. worked two full-time jobs. The family lived a middle-class lifestyle in the suburbs. Their home had three bedrooms, two bathrooms, a basement, and a pool. Jackie enjoyed being a wife and a stay-at-home mom. She had everything she ever wanted. Jackie loved kids. She and Travis Sr. wanted a large family and were trying to have another baby. She'd gotten lonely when the kids started school. She started experiencing the empty-nest syndrome. Jackie started volunteering at schools, churches, and a daycare. And she attended girls' club meetings.

Travis Sr. worked so much that he never had the time to spend with his family. One night while leaving one job to go to another, he fell asleep and lost control of his Lexus. He crossed over into oncoming traffic. His car ran directly into a transfer truck. Travis died instantly. On impact, it had severed his head from a steel beam that was on the back of the truck.

This news was too devastating for Jackie. She suffered a nervous breakdown. The news about their father's death wasn't as devastating to the boys. They showed no emotions. Life went on as unusual. The boys convinced themselves that their father was working his two jobs like before. He had rarely been at home, and when he was at home, he'd been so tired he would stay in his bedroom and catch up on his sleep. The boys had never interacted with him, so to them, pretending their father was still working his jobs was easy, and that's what they told their friends until they were old enough to know better.

Jackie was lost without Travis Sr. He was her soul mate. They had never planned for the what-ifs. They'd never discussed what to do if one of them died before the other. They were young and believed they had their whole lives ahead of them. There was no money saved. They had lived from paycheck to paycheck just to keep up their lifestyle. Jackie received Travis Sr.'s life insurance check. It didn't make her a rich woman.

Two years after her husband's death, Jackie hit a financial low. The monthly social security check was not enough to keep up the same lifestyle. They would have to downgrade—move into something less expensive and sell one of the cars. Jackie and the boys moved out of their suburban home and into a two-bedroom, one-bathroom apartment on Baker Street.

Moving into the Hamptons was not a choice Jackie wanted to make. All her husband's hard work and sacrifice to keep them safe and out of the projects had died with him. Now Jackie was responsible for protecting and keeping her boys grounded and safe. She had to make sure Travis and Jamal didn't get caught in a negative environment that would influence them—the environments that she'd heard were prevalent in the Hamptons.

Jackie hoped she could make a difference in the Hamptons. She wanted to make the neighborhood a better place to live in and restore stability, peace, and trust. She was determined to make the Hamptons a safe place to live. She didn't know how. But she was determined to accomplish this.

They lived in a fickle area, where you were judged by your looks and talent. This was going to help Jackie with these kids. Jackie's pretty face, sexy looks, and Tina Turner legs made her an instant popular hit. Travis and Jamal were popular with the girls because they were "new meat." The guys accepted them because they were good at football. Jackie's pleasant personality and patience with people made them gravitate to her.

Jackie wanted to get to know the kids on Baker Street, so she threw her first outdoor barbeque. Free food and loud music were featured on the advertisement asking all to come, which they did. Just about everyone in the Hamptons was at the barbecue. The party got out of control. Jackie couldn't contain the kids. They were rude, pushy, and disrespectful. This let Jackie know she had her work cut out for her. She was determined to make an impact on these kids' lives. Her sons' future depended on it. She didn't want her sons' lives to get derailed because of where they lived and whom they befriended.

Chapter Two

Kathy and Michelle

Kathy was Jackie's best friend. Her daughter, Michelle, was dark complexion, tall, skinny, and plain-looking. She wore thick glasses and had braces on her teeth. Her waist-length hair was always in ponytails or braids. Michelle's IQ was well over genius level. She was one of the smartest, most gifted kids in the United States.

Kathy and her husband divorced because outsiders had interfered in their life. Her family and friends were jealous of her. She had a good, stable relationship, and they didn't. They kept telling her that Tony was no good and that he was cheating on her. Tony traveled a lot with the military. He took his family with him most of the time, but there were a few occasions when Tony had to travel alone. This would upset Kathy. She started believing the gossip her family and friends were telling her.

Tony wanted to move Kathy far away from her family and friends. He knew they were causing the problems in their marriage. Kathy refused. Kathy's mother told her that Tony wanted to isolate her from her family so he could mistreat and take advantage of her. This was the furthest thing from the truth. Tony loved Kathy and Michelle. He would do anything to keep his family intact. Kathy didn't realize this. Her family and friends were sabotaging her relationship. They were jealous. She had what they wanted. It was hard to find a decent man. A couple of her friends came on to Tony. Kathy refused to believe him when he'd told her about their advances. Kathy always took her friend's side over Tony.

Tony tried to convince Kathy that he had always been faithful. He never looked at another woman. The bad-mouthing, lies, and gossip eventually won. Kathy left her husband and moved in with her mother. Tony took the breakup hard. He fell on his knees, crying and begging Kathy not to leave him. He did everything he could to get her back. When Tony was growing up he had enjoyed watching family sitcoms on TV like *Leave It to Beaver or Father knows best*. He wanted a life like that. He wanted to be a family man. Nothing he did convinced Kathy to change her mind. She was enjoying the single life, hanging out with her friends. Every weekend, they went to clubs and met different men.

When Tony found out that Kathy was seeing other men, he was crushed. He retaliated by suing for custody of Michelle. Tony strongly believed that Michelle needed to be raised by both parents. He didn't want another man around his daughter or putting his hands on her. The custody fight got uglier when Tony heard that Kathy was seriously involved with another man. Tony had been holding onto the hope that he and Kathy would get back together.

The judge ruled in Kathy's favor. He said that Michelle needed a stable environment and she wouldn't have that with Tony because he traveled a lot. Tony cried a lot. For up to two years, Tony kept asking Kathy about getting back together. She refused each time. She enjoyed his begging and wanting to get back with her. It made her feel good about herself. She was confident that he was always going to be there when she ready.

Tony missed Kathy and wanted to hold her in his arms and make love to her again. His body craved her so much that it hurt. After being rejected numerous times, he realized it was time to move on. He needed to be loved. He met Brook, a quiet, shy, attractive woman, in church at a singles meeting. They dated, got married, and had twin boys. Michelle was at the wedding and the birth of the twins. Tony and Brook let Michelle cut the umbilical cord so she could have a special bond with the twins. Michelle was excited to be a big sister. She loved her new family. They were all she could talk about. Brook and the boys were just as crazy about her. They all looked forward to Michelle's visits. Tony was the happiest he ever been.

Kathy got a little jealous when Brook had the babies. She tried not to show it. Kathy thought she would be the one remarried first. Kathy whispered to herself, "Being single is not what it's cracked up to be." Tony was happy, and she was depressed. He was financially secure and owned his own home; she was barely making it and lived with her mother. Tony had two cars and a truck, while Kathy shared her mom's beat-up car. Now that Tony was married, Kathy was beginning to see him for who he was—a good man. She wanted him back and tried to hint around about it.

Tony would never let anyone or anything cloud his judgment. He had told Kathy once, that she was letting her friends influence her. "One day, you going to be all alone. You will never find a good man that going to treat you the way I did."

Once Tony found Brook, he was done with Kathy. He no longer begged or cried for them to get back together. Michelle was still Daddy's little girl. He never missed or was late paying alimony and child support. He sometimes would send extra. Tony and Brook spoiled Michelle. She never had to ask or want for anything. Michelle was always talking about how much fun she had with her daddy and Brook.

Kathy realized she had been a fool for letting Tony go. She blamed her mother and friends for her breakup. Her mother used her. She needed someone to move in with her to help pay bills. Instead, Kathy end up paying all of her mother's bills—mortgage, lights, and water—and buying groceries. Kathy felt trapped. She resented her mother and wanted to move out. Kathy had no money and no back-up plans. Her friends stopped hanging out and didn't come around anymore. They all had boyfriends. Kathy didn't. They didn't want any single woman around their men. Once Kathy's male friends got what they wanted, they moved on. Kathy was heartbroken and lonely often. She couldn't believe she had let Tony go for this life she was living. She felt stupid for not standing by her man. He had warned her about her friends and family.

Although Tony and Kathy's relationship was over, Tony never abandoned Michelle. She would stay with him every summer, Christmas, and spring break. He would visit her on her birthdays and fly in to participate in father and daughter days at her school. Tony put Michelle first. He wouldn't have married Brook if Michelle didn't like her. Tony never gave up trying to persuade Kathy to give him full custody.

Kathy's life was spiraling further down. Nothing had gone right for her since she'd left Tony. When Kathy's mother died, she didn't leave a will. Kathy's three brothers and two sisters had moved into their mother's two-bedroom, one-bathroom house. It became too crowded—six adults and eight kids were stuffed in a small house. Kathy's siblings expected Kathy to continue paying all the bills.

Kathy immediately moved out and made a promise to herself. She was not going to be used anymore by anyone. She applied for emergency housing. The only availability was in the Hamptons. She moved in next door to Jackie on Baker Street. Tony went ballistic when he heard Kathy was moving his daughter into the projects. He tried for custody again and lost. The projects was the only place Kathy could afford, especially on such short notice. She admitted that she'd wasted her alimony and child support on her greedy mother's expenses and that, instead of working, she'd spent her time partying and hanging with her friends. If it wasn't for the extra check Tony sent to their daughter, Kathy didn't know how they would have survived. If Tony ever won custody of Michelle, Kathy would be broke and lost. She couldn't lose Michelle. The Hamptons was not a place she wanted to call home, but home it was for now. The most important thing to Kathy was Michelle. Her number one priority was keeping Michelle protected and safe.

Tony had already told Kathy that if anything ever happened to Michelle, he would kill her. Tony tried one last time for custody. He was denied again. He got tired of the judge denying his request. The judge stated that, as long as Michelle was not being mistreated, a daughter needed to be with her biological mother.

Chapter Three

Hollywood and her mother, Victoria

Victoria was an airline stewardess for a major airline. She was a tall, beautiful African American woman. She captured the attention of men and women with her presence. She had been in commercials for shampoo and hair removal products. Victoria wanted to be an actress or to settle down and marry someone rich. After nine years of traveling all over the world, she was ready to settle down in one place. She dated actors and businessmen. Her relationships with these men were short-term. The men dated her because they wanted to be seen with a beautiful woman on their arm. She was getting tired of being men's sideshow.

It was no surprise when she fell for a millionaire businessman, Alex. She fell in love from the moment she met him. He promised her the world. In just a few months of romancing, Alex swept her off her feet. He set their love nest up in the exclusive, expensive Woods Towers. He told her to quit her job so he could have full access to her whenever he needed her. He promised to take care of her for the rest of her life. Alex spoiled Victoria with expensive gifts.

Their relationship was in its second year when she got pregnant. Victoria knew Alex would be just as excited as she was once she gave him the news. She started daydreaming about their future together. She couldn't wait to be his wife. She rubbed her belly and whispered, "We are finally going to be a family."

Victoria was the happiest she had ever been. She couldn't control her excitement. And she grew anxious. It had been awhile since she and Alex had been together. Lately, they would get together only once a week or twice a month. Victoria assumed Alex's business meetings were responsible for keeping them apart.

He had told her not to leave messages on his phone and not to e-mail him. Victoria thought he wouldn't mind this time if she called and left a message. She left several messages and e-mails but got no response. She couldn't contain her good news any longer. She was about to burst with excitement. She texted Alex. The first two messages were a buildup before she broke the news. He never texted back or called.

With the third text, she got straight to the point. "We are having a baby. I love you so much. I hope you are as excited as I am. I can't wait to wrap my legs around you. I miss you desperately." She hit send.

The incoming text message was not what she expected. "I remember telling you not to leave any messages on my phone. Are you crazy? I will wire you the money to abort it."

She texted, "I'm going to call you, so pick up the phone. We need to talk."

She called Alex's phone number. He wouldn't answer. His voice mail was turn off. She texted again. -"I'm keeping our baby."

Alex was furious. He didn't want any more text messages, so he decided to call. "We have to take care of this little problem of yours right now. I have a friend. He's a doctor."

"No!" Victoria replied emphatically. "I'm not aborting our baby."

"Yes you are," Alex snapped. "I don't want kids, and you are not trapping me into having one."

"I love you," Victoria said. "I'm not trying to trap you. I want to be the mother of your baby—our baby. We can get married. We can be a family."

"Listen, you fucking black bitch!" Alex snarled. "I don't want a baby. You're going to have that abortion. You better not be pregnant when I get there. If you are … Look, don't make me regret getting involved with you."

"I can't do what you're asking," Victoria insisted. "I won't do it."

"Bitch, I will kill you," Alex shot back. "So help me God. I will chop you up in tiny little pieces and spread your body parts all over the United States. No one will ever find you. You have no one. It will be so easy to make you disappear. No one will ever notice your black ass is missing. No one will come looking for you."

Victoria hung up the phone. Shock and disbelief coursed through her. She was so nervous she couldn't speak. She texted "I don't understand. What's wrong with you?"

Alex called. The phone rang a long time before she got the nerve to pick up. "What is it you don't understand?" Alex said. "I don't want kids. How hard is that to understand? You will have that abortion. The money will be there by 10:30 a.m. tomorrow by express mail."

Victoria was speechless but crying. She couldn't understand where this side of Alex was coming from. The man she thought loved her was now threatening to kill her. Victoria cried and pleaded with Alex. She didn't want to get rid of their baby. She told him he didn't have to acknowledge the baby. She was still keeping her child regardless of whether he had anything to do with the baby.

Alex went into a ruthless rage. "Listen, you black bitch. You are not forcing a baby on me. You have twenty-four hours to get rid of that thing inside you."

Crying, Victoria screamed, "How can you call our baby a thing?! What's wrong with you? I thought you loved me. You said you loved me! Why are you doing this to us? I love you so much. I want us to be a family. I know you love me. Please don't do this to us. I know you don't mean what you're saying. I want to keep my baby—our baby. This is our love child."

Alex interrupted, "Damn it! Stop! Just stop and shut the hell up. You do this, and it will be the end of us."

"No," Victoria pleaded. "No; you don't mean that. This doesn't have to be the end of us. We can be together. The baby won't change anything."

Alex yelled, the anger in his voice growing, "You just don't get it, do you! I don't want a damn baby. And I don't want a black ass nig …"

She cut him off before he could finish. "Why are you saying these awful things to me? I don't know you anymore."

"This is the last time we're discussing this," Alex insisted. "The money will be there tomorrow by 10:30 a.m. I can't be with you. I have a business meeting. Remember what I told you earlier. You better take care of it or else."

Victoria was speechless and afraid. She was shaken up. She knew Alex meant what he said. She had never seen this side of him before. She had to act quickly. She needed to know what deep, dark secret Alex was harboring.

Victoria had never had much luck with men. She'd though Alex would be different. This was the longest relationship she'd ever been in. He treated her like gold. She didn't understand what had gone wrong. How could he be a loving, affectionate person one day and talk about cutting her into pieces the next day? Could he be serious? Who was Alex Fitzgerald? She wanted answers and she needed them now.

She used the money Alex wired her to hire a private investigator. The news he gave her wasn't good. Alex was married with two kids—a son close to her age and a daughter who had just turned one. The most disturbing news was that Alex was a supremacist—a racist and a bigot.

"Damn you!" Victoria shouted. "You white motherfucker. This black woman was good enough to fuck but not good enough to have your baby. I hope you riot in hell. You are a liar, a cheat, and an asshole. I hate you. I can raise my own baby. I don't need you or any man to help me rise my baby. My baby and I going to be just fine. Fuck you, Alex Fitzgerald!" Victoria was distraught. She yelled, though no one was there to listen, as she packed her suitcases.

She didn't see how she'd miss this side of Alex. She hadn't seen the signs that he was married. She was so wrapped up in him that she'd missed the signs. She promised herself she would never trust a man again. She was done with all men. She couldn't forgive Alex for his deceitfulness. She sobbed. She was hoping this was a bad dream and she would soon wake up from her nightmare.

Victoria closed her eyes and said a silent prayer. "Oh God, why do I still want this man? Please forgive me. Please, God, let Alex love our baby. Our baby doesn't need to suffer and live poorly because of our sins. I didn't know he was married. Please don't let my baby pay for our sins. Please give Alex a compassionate heart so that he will do right by our baby and give our child what rightfully belongs to him or her. Please. God, please have mercy on my unborn child. Amen."

Victoria wondered if Alex had ever loved her. She questioned herself. She wondered whether Alex would carry out his threat against her once he found out she was still pregnant.

She wanted him to call and say that everything was all right. But she couldn't wait around to find out if he would change his mind.

She left town quickly before he arrived. She needed more money. She couldn't sell the cars or the house as everything was in his name. She had some money saved and withdrew her 401(k). She contacted a local church that helped abused women in crises. The church workers moved her from California to North Carolina.

The only emergency housing availability was in the Hamptons. Victoria felt she was too good for the projects. She became argumentative with the office staff. She thought they could put her in a home that was affordable and upscale. She kept telling the office personnel that she was not moving in that ghetto slum. The staff gave her an ultimatum. "Move into the Hamptons or go find your own damn place." Those were the exact words of the staff member who spoke with her. They were sick of her by now.

Victoria knew no one in North Carolina, and she had no other place to go. She had no choice. She moved into the Hamptons on Baker Street. She changed her last name and social security number. Victoria had a beautiful, healthy baby girl she name Hollywood—because she looked like a movie star.

Victoria was conceited, and her daughter was growing up to be the same. When Hollywood was old enough, she became obsessed with Halle Berry. She had her name legally changed to Hallie Barry. Hallie was just as beautiful and sophisticated as Halle Berry. Victoria and Hallie had the essence of class. They look and acted like movie stars. They were too good for and better than everyone who was not in there circle. They soon got the reputation of being called stuck-up.

Chapter Four

Vera and Family

Vera had three kids. The youngest was her daughter, Lisa. Of her two sons, Randy was the younger. The oldest, Ron was named after his father, Ronnie.

Ron will grow up to be the finest and most popular guy around. He was athletic and good at all sports. He excelled in football. Everyone wanted to be him, and all the girls wanted him. Vera's children had different fathers. Only one of those men had shattered her heart to pieces. His name was Ronnie. She had fallen for Ronnie hard.

She knew he was engaged to another woman when she set her sights on him. She threw herself at him anyway. She wanted more than a sexual encounter. Vera wanted to be his wife and have him all to herself. There was nothing she wouldn't do to get her man. No rules applied. He was worth more to her than any million-dollar lottery ticket. She did whatever it took. She was his freak in the bedroom. She spent her hard-earned money buying him clothes and jewelry and taking him out to eat.

Nothing changed. He was still engaged to another woman. Vera got pregnant intentionally. Ronnie had a beautiful heart. He was honest with the women who wanted to get involved with him. He let them know he was getting married so they wouldn't expect anything more. He believed in being honest and that everyone would be responsible for his or her own feelings. He didn't lead anyone on, so no one would get hurt. When he felt a woman was getting serious, he would break it off.

Vera was different from the rest of the women. He broke things off with Vera a number of times. She would always find her way back into his life. She seduced him, and he would give in. She gave him the best sex he'd ever had. He had feelings for Vera, and he would have considered her the one. But Ronnie's rule was that his main lady had to have gone to college. Being good in bed wasn't enough for Ronnie. He needed the whole package—smart, hardworking, positive attitude, college degree, and good in bed. What Vera had to offer wasn't enough to make him leave his fiancé—not even when Vera pronounced her pregnancy.

Ronnie told Vera he would stand by whatever decision she made. Ronnie's fiancée, Nina, was forgiving, and the wedding went on as scheduled. Ronnie supported Vera's pregnancy and paid all the medical expenses. He was in the delivery room and cut the cord when Vera gave birth. He was a proud father to a healthy, beautiful eight pound nine ounce boy. Vera named the baby after Ronnie—Ronnie Jr. They called the baby Ron for short.

Ronnie made sure his son was well provided for. He spent time with him. While Ronnie was spending time with his son and beaming about having a son, Vera was assuming she and Ronnie were a couple. She believed Ronnie was going to leave his wife for her.

Ronnie was a good-looking, smart young man with his master's degree in engineering. He had a good-paying job, and Nina was a registered charge nurse. Nina, being a Christian, was a forgiving and friendly woman. She loved baby Ron as if he were her own. Although she wasn't ready to have her own baby, she helped Ronnie with Ron Jr. Nina didn't believe in divorces. She knew she had a man every woman wanted. This was a turn-on. She knew Ronnie's women envied her. She was the one he'd chosen to marry.

In the middle of their lovemaking, Nina would make Ronnie tell her about his sexual encounters with the women he'd been with. She wanted all the details. This got her aroused. She would have him simulate the exact things he did to them with her. Their lovemaking was wild and hard. She would scream and shake like an earthquake when they reached her climax. They became weak and couldn't move for hours. She would never call herself one, but Nina was a freak in the bedroom. The only time she got a real good climax was when Ronnie was having an affair.

Nina was in love and the happiest she'd ever been. She knew Ronnie felt the same way. She was never threatened by any of his girlfriends or by Vera with her baby. She knew that Vera had gotten pregnant intentionally and that she was still trying to use her baby to come between them. Nina knew Vera didn't stand a chance. She didn't have an education or a career.

Nina and Ronnie planned on having kids in the near future, once they were financially secure. Taking care of baby Ron gave them practice.

Vera discovered that Nina was playing mama to her son. She was hurt. She cried so hard her eyes swelled shut. Vera was still holding onto the hope that Ronnie would be her man. She was addicted to him. She couldn't let go. Ronnie was the best lover she'd ever had. When he cut her off sexually, she went crazy. She wouldn't eat or sleep. She stalked him and begged him to make love to her. She sometimes went into a rage. She wanted any kind of relationship with Ronnie, just as long he was still a part of her life. She would settle for just sex.

After Vera got pregnant, Ronnie wouldn't have sex with her anymore. He believed she would try to get pregnant again. His decision hurt her. She wanted to hurt him for rejecting her. She hated Nina. She wished for Nina's death.

Once Vera realized her baby was giving Ronnie and Nina ideas of having their own baby, she took quick action. She knew Ronnie loved his son. She took their baby away so he couldn't see him again. She hoped he would miss his son enough to leave his wife and be with her. Vera moved far away.

Ronnie didn't know where to send the child support checks. As time went by, Ronnie stopped searching for his son. He turned his attention to his wife, who was pregnant and having difficulties.

Nina watched the suffering her husband was going though missing his son. She decided it was time for them to have their own baby. His pain and suffering was her pain and suffering. She wanted to fill his life with joy and laughter again. She wanted to see his face light up like it did when baby Ron was around.

Vera heard through the grapevine that Ronnie and Nina had welcomed a healthy nine pound baby boy name Ronnie Lawrence II. The news became too much for Vera. She blacked out. She still carried a torch very deeply for Ronnie, and all the pain and hurt came flooding back. The tears she'd harbored inside came pouring out again. The sadness and hurt this time was different. The hurt were more intense. She felt like she had lost Ronnie forever. Vera went into a deep depression. Ronnie was the only man she'd ever loved; he was the only one who could complete her. Vera lost all sense of reality. Nothing seemed to matter anymore. She tried to commit suicide. She took a handful of barbiturates and lay unconscious on the floor.

When four years old Ron discovered her lying lifeless, he called 9-1-1. EMTs rushed Vera to a nearby hospital. It was a near-death situation. The medical staff revived her.

Vera was never the same after that night. She was angry and depressed all the time. Her state of mind affected her everyday living. She was placed on mind control medications. Vera couldn't stay focused long enough to keep a job. She slept with any man who wanted her. Vera had two other kids. All three had different fathers.

Social services helped Vera get an apartment in the Hamptons, rent free, on Baker Street. She still couldn't get Ronnie out of her mind. All the mind-control medication and alcohol didn't drown him out of her mind. She couldn't stop envisioning him making love to Nina. It hurt her so much to know that Nina and Ronnie were happy, in love, and living like the Huxtables. The pain was intense and too much to bear. It was like an arrow shooting through her heart. She couldn't escape being reminded of Ronnie. She tried.

Her son was growing up to look just like his father. She resented her own flesh and blood. She blamed Ron Jr. for everything that had gone or would go wrong in her life. She made sure he would suffer for it. She was going to make Ron regret ever calling 9-1-1 to save her life. Vera would rather be dead than live without Ronnie. She didn't care what happened to her. She started living a reckless lifestyle. She hoped one of her one-night stands would be a serial killer and finish her off.

Chapter Five

Geraldine and Donnie

Geraldine was a quiet, shy woman whose paranoia had gotten the best of her. She was always suspicious of her surroundings and everyone. She couldn't hold a public job. She jumped and screamed when she heard loud noises. She was afraid some crazy person would start shooting anyone in sight—at the mall, on the job, or wherever she might be at the time. Geraldine was afraid to go around large crowds. She never stuck around when a fight or argument broke out. She never dated. She was afraid her date might kill her.

She moved in the Hamptons based on her mental inability. Her social worker and psychologist worked to get her a job and an apartment. They were rehabilitating her, so that she could live a normal, healthy life. Geraldine was afraid to socialize with people. Her psychologist got her a job as a personal nanny. The child she took care of was the son of a client and a friend of her psychologist. Knowing Geraldine could do the job and wanting her to interact with people, the psychologist recommended Geraldine.

Geraldine started when the little boy, Donnie, was two. A Caucasian family, Donnie's parents and grandparents were multimillionaires. Donnie was the only heir. Geraldine practically raised him. She was a good nanny, and she was overprotective of her charge. Donnie thought of her as his mother. His parents traveled a lot. When they were away, Geraldine kept Donnie at her apartment on Baker Street.

She was afraid to stay in the mansion. It was huge. She was constantly checking windows and doors to make sure they were locked. The neighborhood was dark and quiet. Houses were too far apart from each other. She kept Donnie with her at her apartment, and he loved it there. He like being around the people in the Hamptons, and they liked him. He was just as much a part of the projects as the people who lived there full time.

Donnie was raised around all African Americans throughout his childhood. He started believing he was a light-skinned African American. He wore baggy pants, and his long, blond hair hung in dreadlocks. In the Hamptons, no one cared about your race. You just had to be cool and good at football. Everyone was crazy about Donnie. He was cute and wild. He kept plenty of money and shared it with his close friends. Donnie couldn't wait for his parents to leave town so he could go home with Geraldine. Geraldine's place was more fun than the big, empty home where he lived.

Donnie made his parents take him out of private school so he could go to public school where his friends went. Sometimes he rode the bus with them. Donnie's neighborhood, the Manor Estates, was boring. No one interacted with each other. The neighborhood association did not allow kids to play outside, sit on the porch, or make noise. There were no neighborhood parks to play basketball in. There were many more strict rules. Houses were so far apart from each other you had to get in your car and drive to visit your next-door neighbor. It was dark, quiet, and boring.

The Hamptons was the opposite. Outside was all lit up, and someone was always doing something twenty-four hours a day. The Hamptons was like New York City; it never slept. People hung out playing basket ball until three o'clock in the morning, music playing loud. Some people never sleep they hung out all night long.. On a hot night, you could find someone sitting on the porch, or at the park playing basketball or just chilling with his or her mate. To Donnie, this was the life—it offered excitement. He loved the projects. There was never a boring minute in the Hamptons. Donnie was always saying that when he grew up, he was moving to the Hamptons.

Still a child, Donnie didn't realize that when he grew up, he would be worth well over a billion dollars. He also didn't know he was the only son of multimillionaires and the only grandson of billionaires. His parents were always away mingling and partying with the "upper-class, society types".

Donnie's grandparents wanted Donnie to live with them. They spoiled and showered him with material things. He didn't like all the fuss over him. Donnie's birthdays, Christmas, and Thanksgiving were the only occasions on which all his family, including Geraldine, spent time together. When school was out, they took a long family vacation together. Donnie's parents showed their love with money and gifts. Whatever his parents or his grandparents gave him, Donnie was generous with the money. He paid for his friends to go to the movies or hang out at the mall, shopping and eating.

Part II

The Present

Chapter Six

Jackie's Place

Jackie was the glue that kept the neighborhood together. She was likable and respected. She was always saying, "Adults need to show respect to their kids in order to get respect. They shouldn't do drugs or let different men come in and out of their lives. Kids see too much today. They have to grow up fast and raise themselves because their parents are too busy for them."

Jackie was always there for her children and the other neighborhood children. She taught the illiterate to read. She gave them advice on just about anything they asked her. She talked to them about the importance of safe sex and a good education. Jackie wasn't afraid to get down and dirty. She played football, basketball, and soccer. She got tackled just like the boys. She didn't care about breaking her manicured nails or getting her salon hairdo messed up.

Kathy wasn't the type to get dirty. She stayed on the sideline and watched. Jackie would have Kathy get the grill started for the cookout after a game. Jackie's apartment became the hangout for all adolescents. Everyone liked her. The teenagers said she was hip and cool, and they wished their mother was like her.

Travis, Jamal, Ron, Randy, Lee, Chris, Eric, Donnie, and Sean were considered the popular guys in school. Ronnie Jr. friends called him Ron. He was the most popular of them all. He was tall and had a chocolate smooth complexion; a muscular build; thick, curly eyelashes; and perfect, white teeth. When he smiled girls melted. Everyone treated Ron like an A-list celebrity—everyone except Hallie. Ron was the spitting image of his father. He was even better looking than Ronnie. He wasn't vain. Jamal, Ron, Lee, and Donnie were the best of friends. They were like brothers. They tried out for the same sports teams. They were always together when they weren't with their girlfriends.

Ron didn't realize he was the leader of the pack. Everyone wanted to hang or just be seen with Ron. Teachers and parents liked him. They all believed Ron was going to put their school on the map. They believed he was going to bring their high school football to Division One and win. Then they could qualify for a grant to build a betters stadium. Ron wasn't aware of his influence and popularity. All the guys in their clique were athletes. They were always trying out for the same sports team Ron was trying out for. Girls threw themselves at the guys. Ron, Donnie, Eric, and Lee dated different girls and refrained from getting serious with any of them. They tried to convince Jamal he needed to date different girls.

Jamal claimed to be in love with Hallie, and they were already talking about marriage. He wouldn't even look at another girl. Hallie was considered the prettiest and most popular girl in school—some said in the city. She had her girl group, and the girls in it were all pretty and stuck-up.

Jackie disapproved of her son's involvement with Hallie. She knew Jamal and Hallie were too young to be so serious. She made her son aware of how she felt, and Jamal told Hallie how his mother felt about their relationship. That was one of the reasons Hallie didn't like Jackie. Jackie hoped that, once Jamal went away to college, this relationship would be over for good. She never cared for Hallie because the girl was bossy, snobbish, and spoiled. Hallie got her way with her mama, her friends, and Jamal. She made Jamal look humble and like less than a man in front of his friends and family.. All of Jamal's friends and family disapproved of Hallie. He acted henpecked. He jumped whenever she told him to.

Jamal worshiped Hallie. He was obsessed with her beauty. He believed having the prettiest girl in school made him look good. He liked showing Hallie off and knowing men wanted her and couldn't have her because she belonged to him. It made him feel important.

Hallie grew up looking like a movie star. She was conceited. She would get jealous if anyone else got a compliment or attention over her. This was the second reason why Hallie was jealous of Jackie. Jackie got attention and compliments for her shape and legs. If God were to make the perfect woman, it would be Hallie. Her conceited, arrogant attitude was her only flaws. Her conceit showed. She wore tight-fitting cloths, revealing blouses, and very short dresses, and she didn't mind walking around in her bikini and high heels. She liked to draw attention. Hallie had the personality of her mother.

Victoria only socialized with people outside of the projects. She was too ashamed to tell her friends and coworkers where she lived. Victoria thought she was better than anyone in the Hamptons. She considered her neighbors lower class. She taught Hallie to marry for money and do whatever it took to get out of the projects. Hallie believed Jamal had potential. He was her link to getting out of the projects once he went pro. Jamal was her only way out because everyone else could see right through her. She knew Jamal was weak for her. She would brag to her friends that she could make him do whatever she wanted.

Hallie didn't like Jamal hanging with his boys, especially Ron. She knew Ron to be a player and a bad influence on Jamal. Ron was giving Jamal advice on how dirty Hallie was, saying that she made him look henpecked in front of his boys. Hallie knew this because Jamal told her what Ron said. This information made Hallie hate Ron. Hallie did go off on Jamal in front of his friends. She liked to argue, but Jamal didn't. He would throw his hands up and walk away.

Jamal knew Hallie was poison, but he was addicted to her. He had been a virgin when he'd gotten involved with Hallie. She did things to him that he never imagined could be done to a man.

Vera, Ron, Randy, and little Lisa's mother, was always hooking up with men she found on the Internet. She would leave for a good length of time without telling anyone where she was going or how long she would be gone. If the relationship didn't work out, she always came back to her rent-free apartment. She would just start all over again on the online dating services. She would leave her kids to take care of themselves. Vera didn't care about anyone but herself. In her search for a husband one criteria was important—her man must have his own home. This would be her way out of the projects.

Vera didn't worry about the kids having enough food in the house or if they would be taken good care of. While she was away, she never called to check on them or asked anyone else to do so.

Ron was used to his mother disappearing, so he made sure he took the responsibility of caring for his siblings. Little Lisa loved her big brother, and Randy looked up to Ron. If Randy or Lisa needed anything, they would go to Ron before they would go to Vera. Little Lisa and Randy called their mother by her first name, Vera; Ron called her Mother.

One morning before leaving for school, Ron gave his mother a peck on the cheek. She took a frying pan and hit him across the back with it. "You ugly motherfucker," she screamed, "don't you ever touch me again. Your damn mouth has been on your damn whores. I hate your stupid ass. You just like your no-good ass daddy. He didn't want you. That's why he married that bitch. He told me to kill you," she lied. "I should have. Your damn daddy ain't shit. I hate you and him."

That was the first and last time he gave his mother a kiss. He knew his mother didn't care for him, but he didn't understand how a mother could hate her own flesh and blood. She made it clear that she hated him and how much she hated him. Ron continued trying to be the son she would approve of.

Jackie was always there for Ron and his siblings. She made sure they got home-cooked meals every day, never missed a day of school, did their homework on time, and were in bed early on a school night. Jackie gave them motherly love, something they never got at home. While Vera was away, Jackie moved Vera's kids in with her.

Neighbors could tell when Vera was away. It was quiet. When she was home, she was always screaming and cussing. She called Ron names, threw things at him, and fought him. There were times Jackie would have to come to Ron's rescue and take him out of that environment. Ron never defended himself against Vera. He didn't want to hurt her. He just blocked the blows long enough to get away from her.

Randy hated Vera's tirades against Ron, he would get upset and angry. He even, at one time, plotted to kill Vera while she slept. Ron talked him out of it. Randy couldn't understand why Ron was overprotective of Vera. Randy hated her and wished she would go away and never return.

Little Lisa cried when Vera left when she was younger, but that soon faded. She cried more for her big brother when he left for school or to go on a date. Sometimes he took her on his dates. She enjoyed them and had a lot of fun. Ron's girlfriends would buy little Lisa clothes and toys. They'd do her hair. They'd go to Burger World, the zoo, the circus, and the fair. Ron spoil little Lisa, and Lisa looked forward to Vera leaving so she could go with her brother on his dates.

Ron always worried about his mother when she was away. He loved her no matter how badly she treated him. No one knew anything about the men she met on the Internet. Once she connected to one that she liked, she would take the Greyhound to stay with her new man until he put her out. If she was murdered on one of her vacations, they may never find her body or learn who'd killed her. That's why Ron worried when she left.

Randy, on the other hand, prayed for the day Vera didn't return. Then, just maybe, Jackie would adopt them and they could know what it was like to have a real, normal, healthy family.

Geraldine felt safe in her own environment. She raised Donnie in the Hamptons. When he became a teenager, he was sporting blond dreadlocks, baggy pants, oversize shirts, and every name brand tennis shoe that existed. Donnie's girlfriends were African American. He was always sitting between some girl's legs getting his hair braided. All Donnie's friends were African American. He also thought he was too.

His parents never questioned Donnie's personality changes. They assumed it was a teen phase and he would eventually grow out of it. His parents wanted Donnie to experience all cultures. They knew it would benefit his political career in the future. Donnie didn't know it, but his parents and grandparents already had his future mapped out for him. Donnie had his own dreams, and one of them was being a famous rap singer—partying and, in his own words, "banging all the whores I can get."

Chapter Seven

Getting the Day Started

Every morning, Jackie was up by 5:00 a.m. She made sure her kids and Vera's kids were up, fed, and ready for school.

Jackie and Kathy worked together. They would leave before the kids. They were best of friends and lived next door to each other. They did everything together and shared their personal secrets with each other. They worked part-time as customer service representatives. They trusted each other. Before work, they would stop at a coffee house to enjoy coffee and bagels. This was their private time to chat without interference from others. People were always in and out at Jackie's apartment. Although the coffee house was full, it was still a peaceful time for them to talk and catch up on gossip, sex, and men without being interrupted.

Michelle was always around. Kathy never let her out of her sight. She was very protective of Michelle. So when Jackie and Kathy got together, they had to watch what they said.

The coffee house was there hangout. They almost never ran into anyone they knew from the Hamptons. But one time, they saw Victoria with her Caucasian friends. She smiled and spoke like she didn't know them. After that day, they never saw Victoria at that coffee house again.

Kathy and Jackie liked staring at the people who came in and out of the coffee shop. They noticed the ones who came in as couples. "Jackie, do you ever miss having a man around?" Kathy asked.

"Sometimes," Jackie replied. "I'm looking around here and wonder where these women are getting their men from."

"I know," Kathy agreed. "I've never seen so many people with mates. When I see couples kissing and acting like they're so in love, I'm wondering, will they be together a year or two from now?"

Jackie sighed. "I sometime wonder that myself. Relationships don't last; marriages don't last. I'm afraid to fall in love again. Do you want to get married again?"

Kathy thought for a moment. "I wish I hadn't been so stupid by letting Tony go," she told her friend. "He was a good husband to me. The only sex I get now is when he comes to visit his daughter."

Jackie looked shocked. "What! Are you saying you and Tony are doing it?"

"Yep, we are," Kathy replied.

"That sly dog. He's cheating on his wife." Jackie was laughing and sliding her chair up closer so she could hear more clearly. There were many sidebar conversation drowning out their conversation. "How long has this been going on?" she asked.

"For a couple of years. I needed sex so badly. So I seduced him. I just wish we could hook up more often."

"Do you think he still has feelings for you?" Jackie asked.

"He made me promise not to tell anyone, not even Michelle," Kathy answered. "He would have a stroke if he knew I told you. He made it perfectly clear that this was all it would be between us—just sex. He reminded me that I had my chance and blew it. I let him go, and he was the best thing I would ever have in my life."

"He said that to you?" It was a rhetorical question, and the women sipped their coffees quietly before Jackie added softly, "Damn! He's acting just like the rest of these no-good assholes out here. How did that make you feel when he told you that?"

"It hurt some," Kathy said matter-of-factly. "But he's right. He told me I hurt him more than I can imagine and that he could never trust me. And he also made it clear he has a good wife and he's not leaving her for anyone."

"Oh—really—how did that make you feel?" Jackie persisted.

"It hurts," Kathy admitted. "But that's the kind of guy Tony is. I did hope we could get back together."

Jackie eyed her friend. "Kathy, you don't strike me as the type to break up a marriage. You're better than that. If your heart can't handle a casual affair, then you need to break it off and buy you a toy."

"I can handle it," Kathy replied. "I know where I stand."

Jackie sipped her coffee and grinned at her friend. "So is the sex the same or better?"

"He's better, girl," Kathy replied right away. "He won't do oral sex on me because we're not married."

"Well, I can relate to that," Jackie said. "If I had a man, there'd be two things I wouldn't forgive him for—getting another woman pregnant and going down on her."

"We did each other when we were married; now he just wants me to do him."

"You're crazy if you're doing him and he won't do you," Jackie said.

"Yeah, you're right," Kathy agreed. "But if I don't give him oral sex, he won't fuck me. He told me he doesn't need me; he has a wife. I know I sound stupid, but, Jackie, I get these urges so bad I sometimes want to go online like Vera. I don't know how you can handle being without so long. It's killing me to have to wait for Tony to come in town."

"You know, we need to go out sometimes," Jackie said. "Men don't know we exist because we don't go anywhere to be seen. I do miss a man touching me." She smiled, and added jokingly, "Do you think Tony wants to put out another fire?"

Kathy and Jackie laughed simultaneously. "He's acting like a dog now," Kathy surmised. "He probably would."

"You know I'm kidding," Jackie said. "I don't want a man just for sex. I want to remarry some day. I want a man who has some good qualities about him. He has to be a very caring person, have a lot of patience with kids, and be very active. He can't drink or do drugs. And he's gotta be good in the bedroom."

"That's every woman's ideal man," Kathy replied. "But you forgot the most important thing. He's got to have a job."

"I thought when I said he has to be active that covered that he had to work."

"Some men may consider being active keeping the house clean while the woman works."

Jackie laughed. "You know I better just buy me a toy penis because finding, dealing with, and trying to keep a man is hard work. I might have a better chance of becoming the first black female president than find the man of my dreams."

"Well, like you said, we need to go out more," Kathy said. "I can't wait to replace Tony." Jackie and Kathy laughed again.

"Let's get out of here so we won't be late," Jackie said.

"I'm so glad its Friday. I hate getting up so early," Kathy said as they got in the car.

"You don't like doing anything but sitting on your butt watching the soaps," Jackie teased.

"Damn, I wish I could hit the lottery," Kathy replied. "I hate work."

"You're right," Jackie said, "You should have kept that ex of yours because you're not going to find a man who's going to support you while you sit at home watching TV all day."

Kathy was looking out the car window looking at the sights while Jackie was driving. Kathy said silently as she watched a couple holding hands as they walk. "I wish I could turn back time," she said quietly. "I want my husband back."

*   *   *

When Jackie left for work, Jamal and Travis started their morning getting ready for school. After getting dressed, they would open the doors and windows to blast the radio tuned to their favorite rap station. Everyone on Baker Street could hear the music. This was an invitation to come and hang out before the school bus arrived.

Jamal and Travis's apartment was the hangout for the high school teenagers before the bus arrived. A yeller would watch for the bus to let the insiders know the bus was coming. Kids were gathered in the kitchen, bedrooms, and living room and on the back and front porches. They were everywhere, just hanging out and having fun.

Michelle would sit in a corner reading. She was shy, but she liked the surroundings. She was glad to be around other young people instead of her mother. Jamal and Travis were responsible for Michelle. Michelle's going to public school had almost cost Jackie her friendship with Kathy. Jackie had tried to convince Kathy to let Michelle go to public school and ride the bus. Kathy had argued with Jackie, listing reasons that it was not a good idea. Jackie had counterattacked; persuading Kathy that public school was a perfectly reasonable option for Michelle. Jackie and Kathy had gone back and forth until Kathy had finally caved in. Jackie had promised Kathy that her boys would take care of Michelle. No harm would come to her.

Michelle was not popular; nor was she pretty. She was dark, tall, skinny, and wore thick glasses. Kathy believed that she shielded Michelle from boys by being overprotective. Jackie knew that with the way Michelle looked, no boys would be interested in her. She kept this thought to herself. This was one of the reasons Jackie felt Michelle needed to be around girls she was going to school with. She needed to learn teen culture—how to socialize, dress, wear makeup, and fix her hair.

Michelle was gifted. She had skipped forward in grade level three times. She had taken some college courses and passed. She was tutoring Hallie and some of her friends, along with Jamal. Michelle was a child around all teens. She was smarter than the teachers. Hallie and her friends made an exception with Michelle. She help them with homework so they let her hang around them.. Her IQ was well over gifted level. She was the smartest girl in the United States. She got to meet the president.

Michelle was an introvert. She didn't know how to interact with the teens she was around. She was much younger than her high school peers. No one made fun of Michelle because of her looks. They all liked her and treated her delicately. School was too easy for Michelle. She assisted teachers in grading test papers. She sometimes would teach a class or two. She loved biology and chemistry. Jamal, Travis, Randy, Donnie, and Hallie always got her to help them in subjects they were weak in.

Ron treated Michelle like his baby sister. He would smile and have brief conversations with her about what subjects she was taking and how it felt to be the smartest kid in the world. The other popular guys didn't say anything to her. Jamal and the rest of his clan just asked her in passing if she was all right or told her that, if someone was bothering her, she should let them know. They didn't take the time out to talk or hang out with her. That's why she looked forward to seeing Ron. She blushed when he walked into a room. Her stomach would tinkle. Ron didn't realize his innocent kindness was being mistaken for something else with Michelle. She would rush to get dressed in the mornings so she could go to Jackie's, hoping to see Ron. He didn't always show. Sometimes he would stay at home when he had the place all to himself so he could entertain a girl.

When Ron wasn't around, everyone knew it. When he did show himself, he was always late. The hype and excitement started when Ron arrived. Everyone would be trying to get his attention. The conversation would be about football, girls, music, video games, and school. Michelle noticed the special attention Ron got, especially from girls. She would stare at him as he worked the room. She envisioned herself being his girlfriend. Michelle worshipped Ron. She admired his patience with his sister; she'd watch him walk little Lisa to the bus stop and wait with her until the bus arrived. Ron would do this even when Vera was home. Vera always slept late. She would complain when the music was playing too loudly from her neighbor's. Randy would turn it up louder just to aggravate her.

Ron made sure he wasn't around to get blamed. He would go hang out at the bus stop or shoot some hoops. Michelle would follow him. She watched him shoot some hoops one day. He saw her watching him, so he challenged her to make a basket. She was shy. He took her hands and placed the ball in it. "Bounce it and toss it in that hoop," Ron said. "Go ahead. You can do it."

Michelle bounced the ball and kept missing the basket.

"I'm going to show you how to play basketball," Ron said. "When you grow up, you can have something in common with your boyfriend. Men like women to know a little about sports." Ron had his shirt off, and he jumped up to make the ball go through the hoop.

A crowd soon gathered at the bus stop. Ron started putting his shirt on, and one of his female friends came to assist him. She kissed and licked his chest before she took over buttoning his shirt.

Michelle was hurt and jealous. She felt everything was fine when it was just her and Ron. She knew she had to do something to stand out from the rest of his girlfriends. She knew what she had to do. The first thing she was going to do when she got to school was go to the library and look up everything on basketball—from past to present. She didn't bother to learn how to play. She just wanted all the information she could find on basketball.

Michelle felt she now had something in common with Ron. Next time they were alone she would strike up a conversation about basketball. Michelle couldn't wait to see Ron again. She practiced what she would say and where to start. *Should I name all the top players, starting with the deceased players or talk about how the game was invented?* she wondered. *Or should I mention how much current players gross in a year or game?* Micelle believed Ron would be impressed with her. She closed her eyes and whispered to herself, "I love you, Ron."

Hallie liked having Jamal all to herself. She didn't like sharing him with his mother or his friends. Jamal would be the first to leave the house so he could hang out with Hallie. Hallie didn't like hanging out with Jamal's friends or family. He would leave Travis to lock up and babysit Michelle. At the bus stop, Hallie wanted to be a good distance away from the crowd so they could be alone. They would be kissing and wrapped around each other so close it looked like they were one.

On the bus, they still couldn't keep their hands off each other. They sat up front while their friends sat in the back of the bus. Jamal made sure Michelle sat up front so he could keep his eyes on her.

Donnie, the only white boy on the bus and the loudest, was always in the back. He loved attention and making his friends laugh. Donnie was trying to juggle three girlfriends at a time. All the girls lived in the Hamptons and rode the same bus. There was always a fight over him.

Ron, on the other hand, kept it real with his women. He didn't like drama. His girlfriends would show signs of jealousy, but they knew not to act on it. He would stop messing with them if they did, and none of them wanted that.

Ron was an excellent lover, so the girls waited until it was their turn to be with him. Ron tried to school Donnie on how to handle his women. Donnie liked girls fighting over him. On the days Ron didn't ride the bus, he would get a ride with one of his college friends. The bus driver would wait an extra fifteen minutes and would, sometimes, pull up at Ron's door and honk the horn. The bus driver was a fifty-five year old, overweight, not-so-pretty woman who had a crush on Ron. She let the kids do whatever they wanted on the bus except fight.

Once everyone arrived at school, they all went their separate ways. Jamal and Hallie would walk Michelle to her destination, and then Jamal would walk Hallie to her first period class. They would meet up again during lunch break. They had their special table and certain individuals had a seat saved just for them. No one dared sit in those seats.

Michelle could take her lunch break anytime to accommodate her schedule. She took her break at the same time she knew Ron would. She hadn't talked to him since the day he tried to show her how to play basketball. When she got to the lunch, Ron wasn't there yet. She didn't know she was sitting in Ron's seat. Hallie's best friend, Angela, was already seated at the table. Angela told Michelle that she was sitting in an assigned seat and would have to move.

As Michelle was getting up with her tray, Ron walked up and said, "Hey, beautiful, sit down and join us."

Blushing, Michelle replied, "I don't want to take your seat."

"Nah," Ron insisted, "this seat is yours, baby girl. What's mine is yours. Sit and join us."

Michelle did. She was sitting right next to him. She had knots in her stomach. She couldn't eat. Just sitting near him made her nervous. She listened quietly to the side conversations at the table. Ron and the other guys talked about the football game tonight. They asked each other who was going to the game and what they were doing afterward.

Angela asked Michelle, "Are you coming to the game?"

Ron gave an answer for her in a teasing way. "Nah, she don't need to be corrupted by y'all. You know I know what happens at the games." He smiled as he winked at Michelle.

Michelle blushed as she dropped her head.

Hallie was noticing Michelle blushing.

Jamal asked Ron if he'd found a tutor for chemistry yet.

"No, man," Ron replied. "I really haven't been looking."

"I can help you," Michelle said shyly. "That's one of my favorite subjects."

Hallie interjected. "That's a great idea," she said with a smirk on her face. No one knew what was going on in Hallie's pretty, little. head of hers. Whatever it was, it was not good.

Jamal agreed with Hallie, not knowing her devious little plan. She was always plotting, and Jamal would always be the last to catch on.

Ron didn't want Michelle tutoring him. He preferred someone older, more mature, and ready to put out afterward. He blew her off by telling her he would get back with her. But he never did.

Chapter Eight

The Game

Everyone was excited about the football game tonight. Grandview High had the number one football team in the state thanks to Ron. He was the all-star player on the team. Word got around to keep an eye on number 2. This was the game of the season. Local TV crews were there. If Ron never makes it as an NFL player, he could succeed as a model with his good looks and physique.

The most disappointing part of Ron's life was his mother. She never supported him in anything he did. She never came to any of his games. Vera would tell him he was wasting his time and he was never going to amount to anything. She constantly called him a loser and told him he was dumb or stupid. Ron heard this so often from his mother that he begin to believe it. He did not take any of his popularity or talent seriously.

Vera also told Ron that women—or "whores" as she called them—only wanted him for one thing. This was why Ron never took any girl who came on to him into a serious relationship. He didn't believe anyone could love or care for him.

On the field playing football was the only time Ron felt realness. He only trusted his close friends. Ron was a wide receiver, one of the fastest runners in the state. On that field, he would forget he had problems. Donnie was the quarterback, and Jamal was a halfback.

The excitement in the crowd was growing. Just then, Donnie threw the ball too high. The crowd stood up when they saw Ron jump over one player. But Jamal pretended he had the ball and ran toward the field goal. This confused the opposing team. They left Ron open. Ron caught the ball. His defense covered him. He made a thirty-seven yard run and scored a touchdown. The team was unstoppable. The crowd went wild.

The final score was 21 to 15. Grandview High was number one in the division thanks to Ron. College scouts from all over were there looking at number 2, along with one NFL scout who had heard of this phenomenon—the fastest runner to watch.

Jackie always came to the games just to cheer her babies on. Hallie was a cheerleader. She was the head cheerleader.

Everyone's attention was on the players. People ran down from the bleacher onto the field just to get to their local celebrity players. The attention being on the players and not the cheerleaders didn't sit well with Hallie. She stomped off the field.

Jackie was still sitting on the bleachers with Kathy. Michelle was sitting beside her mother, wishing she could join her friends on the field. Her eyes followed Ron's every move.

Jackie shook her head in disbelief.

Kathy looked at Jackie. "What's wrong?" she asked.

"That damn girl," Jackie replied.

"Who?" Kathy asked.

Jackie answered, "You know who's at it again. Didn't you see her walk off the field in the middle of her cheering act?"

"I don't pay any attention to that heifer," Kathy replied.

"She's so jealous and crazy," Jackie said. "She has to have all the attention on herself. I wish Jamal would see her for who she really is."

"Well you raised him to be good," Kathy said. "It seem good boys get tangled up with bad girls. I believe he can't break it off because he doesn't want to break her heart.

"That girl doesn't have a heart," Jackie retorted. "She only cares about herself. There's a word for people like her."

"Narcissism," Michelle interjected. "She's a narcissist."

Jackie turned to look at Michelle and then at Kathy, as if to say, *Go play, little girl, and get out of grown folk's business.* Jackie stared toward the field and said, "If she cared for Jamal, she would be on that field cheering him on. I just don't get this girl."

"Well get use to her moody ways," Kathy said, "because she going to be your daughter-in-law one day."

"Like hell," Jackie replied. "I'm being patient by keeping out of their business. But once they start planning a wedding, that's when I will intervene. The only way Jamal and that girl will get married will be over my dead body."

"She's no good for him," Kathy agreed. "I feel sorry for Jamal."

"He goes around in a daze when she breaks up with him," Jackie said with a sigh. "She flirts with guys in his face."

"I don't like stuff like that," Kathy said. "That's how people get killed. It's trashy."

Jackie interrupted. "She's trashy. Let's get out of here. I'm throwing a cookout party for the winning team and their friends."

Michelle crisscrossed her way across Kathy and Jackie to get to the crowd on the field. She took a chance by going on the field without her mother's permission. Michelle was just excited about the cookout. If her mother was going to be there, so would she, which meant she would get to be with Ron.

Chapter Nine

The Cookout

Jackie, Kathy, and Michelle left the game earlier than the kids so they could prepare for the cookout. They sat the stereo speakers outside and set up some long tables to place the food on, along with chairs Jackie had borrowed from neighbors.

Jackie did all the cooking, while Kathy and Michelle cut and diced the vegetables. The menu consist of hot dogs, hamburgers, and chicken. No alcoholic beverages were serve or allowed. Parents knew that, if Jackie was hosting the party, it would be well supervised. Some of the parents stopped by to get a plate to go.

Some of the teens started dropping in. They were socializing and waiting for the guests of honor—Jamal, Ron, and Donnie. Jackie yelled over the music for Travis's attention. She tried to ask a question. Travis was talking to a girl he met at the cookout, and he didn't hear his mother.

She yelled again. "Has anyone seen Jamal and Ron?" This time she addressed the question to anyone who was listening.

One girl replied, "They left with Donnie and his parents. I forgot to tell you. Donnie wanted him and his friends to ride up in style."

"What kind of style?" Jackie muttered to herself. "What in the world does that boy have his parents doing now?"

"I don't know," the girl said, shrugging her shoulders in a gesture of doubt.

Travis yelled in excitement and pointed, as he and some others jogged to meet Ron, Jamal, Donnie, and couple of other teammates, who were riding up in a limousine. The players got out of the limo. Everyone was chatting, laughing, eating, dancing, and having a good time. They were all trying to get Ron, Donnie, Jamal, and Lee's attention.

Hallie didn't show up for her boyfriend's party. She was home fuming. She wanted Jamal to miss his party and hang out with her at her place. She kept peeping out her window, looking toward the party in Jackie's yard. She got more agitated each time she saw Jamal laughing and having a good time at his party. She paced back and forth, chatting to herself. "I'm going to dump his damn ass. How dare he put that party before me? I know that damn Jackie with her want-to-be-young ass did this intentionally. That bitch doesn't want to see us together."

She peeped out the window and saw Jamal talking to a girl who was a twin. Ron was entertaining the other twin. This made Hallie suspicious. She knew Ron set Jamal up with girls. This made her even more upset. She decided to crash the party. She threw on her fire red lip stick, jeans shorts, red fishnet stockings, stiletto heels, and a bikini top. Hallie's hair hung past her butt. She made sure it was hanging loose and flowing because she knew Jamal loved her hair flowing and loose.

Jackie screamed, "Soooooul train." She jumped up to be the first to go down the soul train line.

Others followed just to strut their stuff down the line. Jackie knew all the latest moods. She blended well with the young teens. Jackie kept herself up. Her body was just as firm as some of the young girls at the party. Her face was smooth and youthful looking.

Some of Travis and Jamal's friends would kid them by saying, "You know one day I'm going be your daddy, and I'll be telling you to go to your room."

They would all get a good laugh from this.

Jackie was getting down on the dance floor, until Hallie strutted in swinging her hips intentionally so she would be noticed. All eyes were on her. Hallie never looked more beautiful and sexy. The girls wanted to be her. The guys wanted to get with her. Hallie was egotistical. Everything had to go her way, no matter who it hurt.

Word got to Jamal that she was there. He quickly jumped up and got away from any females who were hanging around him. He was acting nervous and guilty. Hallie was on the dance floor dancing.Jamal saw how hot she was looking. He couldn't resist, he was all over her.. He kissed her on the neck and ground his genitals against her round, firm behind. Jamal couldn't contain himself. They was grooving with the rhythm of the music. Hallie was grinding her behind with the same beat as Jamal. She took a dip down and slowly rose back up while pressing up against him firmly.

Everyone was watching the sideshow. Some of the guys were drooling at the mouth and saying things like, "Man, I wouldn't mind hitting that. She got a fine rack on her. Jamal is one lucky son of a b. I see why Jamal jump when she say jump."

Jackie was ignoring Hallie and her sideshow. She directed her attention to Kathy. "Come on, Kathy," she said, dancing to a Michael Jackson tune.

"I can't dance," Kathy protested

Jackie danced her way toward Michelle, and grabbing her by the hands, pulled her to the center floor. Michelle didn't have a rhythm. She was rocking back and forth, snapping her fingers to the beat. She was watching and doing everything Jackie was doing. She caught on quickly.

Hallie yelled out while one arm swayed back and forth to the music, "Let's do the hustle."

Everyone fell into position, except Jackie. This was her clue to sit this one out. Miss Diva was on the dance floor and had taken over the party.

Michelle stayed on the dance floor and learned the hustle. She quickly positioned herself next to Ron. She blushed as Ron winked and smiled at her. He grabbed Michelle by the hands to dance. It was innocent. Ron had done the same thing earlier with his sister. He looked at Michelle as a child.

Most of the girls were throwing themselves at him all night while at the party. He liked flirting with them. Ron could get any woman he wanted.

Michelle studied the girls Ron was flirting with, just to get an idea of the type of women he liked. She observed that they were pretty, full breasted, and mature looking; they wore makeup, perfume, and revealing clothes. They could hang out late and could have boyfriends over to their houses. Most importantly, they were putting out. Michelle was innocent, skinny-looking, and flat-chested. At fourteen years old, she knew nothing about sex and had never had a boyfriend. She couldn't go anywhere without her mother. She didn't like having an overprotective parent. Now being in high school, she saw how much fun the older kids were having and the freedom they had to date and go to movies and parties. The only time she had a little bit of freedom was when she is in school and that little bit didn't give her time to act free because everyone who knew her mother looked out for her to make sure she stayed innocent.

Kathy wanted to isolate Michelle from all the fast and loose girls at her school. They were so much older and more experienced than Michelle. Michelle spent her free time on school projects. Michelle wasn't allowed to watch TV—not unless it was the Discovery Channel— or listen to the radio. Kathy and Tony had Michelle participate in as many extracurricular academic pursuits, lessons, and programs as she could fit in. Michelle was fluent in three different languages and was learning two more. She was taking piano and harp lessons.

At night, Michelle would sometimes cry herself to sleep. She would pray to God to make her pretty. She wanted to look like Hallie, Deena, Brenda, or Angela. They were the prettiest girls in school.

The party was winding down; it was getting late. The last song for the night was playing. "Fire" was a sensual song. Girls liked doing the dance called "silhouette" to this song. You didn't need a partner. It was a great song for strippers to do the silhouette. You just moved to the beat in a sexual motion. This dance was usually done in private with a stripper pole.

Kathy was trying to get Jackie's attention with a gesture of her head. When she got Jackie's attention, Jackie turned around and saw Hallie doing the silhouette. She was touching and caressing every curve of her body, pushing her hair up and swinging it from side to side. The last guy who was about to leave decided to hang out until the performance was over. He was hoping he could score big. Everyone knew Hallie was Jamal's girl, but if opportunity presented itself, most guys at the school would have sex with her in a heartbeat. Allegedly, two or more of Jamal's friends already had. When Hallie set out to make Jamal jealous, she would flirt with his friends. Ron was the only one who wasn't interested in Hallie. He valued his friendship with Jamal.

Hallie was really getting into the music, dancing like an erotic stripper. Jamal tried to remove Hallie from the dance floor by grabbing her arm. She jerked away. He couldn't tell Hallie what to do. When he did, she did whatever he'd told her not to do again just for spite. When Jamal got mad at Hallie, because he didn't believe in hitting a female and he didn't like arguing, he would take a long walk just to cool off.

Ron hated Hallie. He knew she was poison to any men she got involved with. He didn't like seeing his best friend constantly being put on a roller coaster ride. Getting involved with Hallie had its consequences. She was very manipulative. She kept Jamal upset and depressed, to the point that it affected his schoolwork. Ron, Travis and Jackie tired to convince him she was not worth it. Jamal wasn't ready to give her up. No matter how many men she been with or how much she hated or degraded his mother, he loved her too much to let her go.

Jackie watched and turned her nose up while Hallie made a fool of her son. "Look at her. She's got everyone looking at her. She's disgusting."

"Anyone doing that dance in public is a whore," Kathy added. "No telling how many men she's messing with."

"Every time we have a good time, she's the only one who spoils it," Jackie lamented. "I'm turning the music off. It's time for everyone to go home anyway." Jackie turned the music off and said loudly, "The party's over, good night." She repeated her announcement again for the partygoers who were still lingering around. She concluded, "Go home. The cheap entertainment is over." Jackie was speaking loudly enough for Hallie to hear.

Jamal walked inside without Ron and Donnie. He was upset and wanted to be alone. Ron met one of his female friends who had a car. They left together. Michelle watched with sadness as Ron drove away. She didn't want to hang around since Ron had left. She told her mother she was tired and was going home. Kathy watched as Michelle made her way home. Kathy stayed around to help Jackie clean up.

Hallie followed Jamal and grabbed him by the arm, pulling him back outside with her. They walked together to her apartment, where she started kissing and undressing him. He was waiting for her to start cussing and yelling, but to his surprise, she didn't. She sprayed whipped cream from his nipples to his private parts. She licked and sucked him like she would ice cream. She had never used the whipped cream on him before. She knew he was enjoying himself by all the loud moaning, groaning, jerking, and twisting he was doing. She had never seen him react like this before. Hallie was casting her spell on him again. When he was just about to reach his peak, he yelled, "Damn, you're good. This is the best. Damn! Damn you! Whoa, baby, I love you. I love you so much.

"I'll do anything for you," he said as he was pushing his entire penis in her mouth and pulling her hair. He added, "You belong to me, baby. I love you. We are forever, no matter what anyone says."

Hallie knew she had accomplished what she'd set out to do. She was satisfied. Her plan had worked.

"Jamal's been over there a long time," Kathy pointed out. "You know what they're doing. Suppose she gets pregnant?"

"I will kill him if he gets her pregnant," Jackie said, Hallie was not the mothering kind. "He better be using a condom for more reason than one." Jackie sounded frantic.

Once everything was clean, Kathy and Jackie called it a night.

Lisa and Randy were staying at Jackie's, since their mother was still gone.

Chapter Ten

The Weekend

It was another weekend—the days everyone looked forward to. There was no school and, for Jackie and Kathy, no work. Everyone would sleep late, except Jackie; this was the time she could catch up on her exercise. She loved to go jogging at the crack of dawn. Travis and Randy would join her because they didn't want her to be alone.

Randy idolized Jackie. He always wished she was his mother. Randy exercised and lifted weights to prepare himself to be just as great as his brother, Ron. Travis was overprotective of his mother. He didn't want her running by herself. He idolized his mother. Travis believed she was the perfect mom. All his friends wanted a mom like her.

Jamal loved his mother too. But Travis felt like Jamal put Hallie over their mom. The first thing Jamal did in the morning when he woke up was call Hallie, and the last thing he did at night before turning in was call Hallie. Jamal and Hallie spent 90 percent of their time talking or being together. The rest was divided among family and friends. They sometimes fell asleep with the receiver still clinched to their ears. When not on the phone with each other, they were always around each other.

Once the morning jog and exercise was done, Jackie would shower and get dressed. She would harass Kathy to get out of bed. Kathy was not an early-morning person; nor did she like exercising. Kathy was not into any physical activities. On nice, warm days she would join Jackie in sitting on the front porch. They liked to people watch; it gave them something to talk about. They loved to gossip, with each other only. Jackie trusted Kathy enough to know that what went in Kathy's ears never got repeated to anyone else. Jackie didn't like the kind of gossip that could ruin someone's reputation. She knew that could lead to some seriously precarious situations. Jackie and Kathy each considered the other her best friends. They never talked ill about each other. They stuck up for each other. They defended each other if someone said something ill about one of them.

Travis didn't bother changing his sweaty clothes. He and Randy decided to hang out at the corner and shoot some hoops with some of their friends. The corner was where all the teenagers hung out. They played basketball, rolled dice, and met girls. They cruised in cars and just hung out with radio blasting. The corner was sometimes called "the block" or "the park." On warm days and nights, cars and motorcycles would be lined up. Drivers wiped down their cars to make them spit shined. If you had a car as a teen, you were in the group. It didn't matter if the car was use or beat up, as long as it ran.

Jackie would sometimes bring snacks to the kids on the corner. They liked seeing her, especially on those hot days. Jackie was always trying to get Jamal to go hang out with his friends at the corner. It was hard to get him off the phone.

"Jamal, get off the phone," Jackie yelled to make sure he heard her since she was on the porch and he was in his bedroom. "It's been three hours. What can you two be talking about this long?"

She waited thirty minutes before she repeated herself. "Get off the phone. Someone else wants to use it sometimes."

Jamal got up and slammed his bedroom door so he couldn't hear his mother.

Hearing the door slam, Jackie went inside. She took the receiver from him and hung it up.

"Why did you do that?" Jamal snapped. "Hallie was on the phone!"

"I don't care," Jackie replied. "I told you to get off the phone. You need to be outside getting some sunshine."

Jamal was furious. He was afraid Hallie was going to be upset with him. "Mom, I need to call Hallie back and tell her what happened."

"Son, stop being henpecked," Jackie said in a calm voice. "You know I love you, and I'm telling you this because I love you. You are too young to be so serious about this girl. This is the only girlfriend you've ever had. You're young. This is the time you should be meeting and dating other girls before getting serious. Get out of the house and go hang at the mall with some of your friends. It's a warm, sunny day. It's Saturday. You can take my car."

When Jackie mentioned the car, Jamal got up, showered, and dressed.

"Thanks, Mom," Jamal said. "I'm sorry if I got upset with you." He kissed her on the cheek, grabbed the keys, and ran to the car.

He started it up, and Hallie ran out her front door and jumped in the passenger seat. Jamal pulled off before Jackie could say a word.

"Damn it!" Jackie swore. "Did you see that? He tricked me. Damn!" Jackie shook her head in disappointment and anger.

"Let's switch the subject before that boy gives you a heart attack," Kathy said. "You ought to know by now he is not going anywhere or doing anything without her. She is putting something on him."

"I hate that he is so weak," Jackie said. "It doesn't look right. She's going to hurt him really bad, and I don't know how he's going to deal with it."

"Just make sure you're around when the chips come falling down," Kathy replied. "And by the way, don't wake me up so early in the morning. I'm sleeping in. I don't have your energy."

"How can you lay in bed all day?" Jackie retorted. "That'd take away my strength, I hope Michelle doesn't grow up to be lazy like you."

"The weekends are for resting," Kathy said.

"The weekend," Jackie said, looking at her friend, "is for fun and catching up on everything that you didn't have time to do during the week."

Kathy met her friend's gaze. "For me, rest is fun. And the weekend is the only time I can catch up on mine. So don't wake me so early." She smiled and added, "Oh, by the way, what are you cooking today?"

"Today is whatever you want day," Jackie said. "Tomorrow will be meatloaf, green beans, and slaw with rolls."

"Well, I'll be up by then," Kathy replied.

"You keep eating and lying around, you're going to get fat."

"You keep cooking like that, you going to lose that pretty figure of yours," Kathy shot back.

"I'm active," Jackie said, "that's how I keep my figure. And when are you going to cook? I can't recall you ever cooking. You always eating over here."

"You cook better than me," Kathy said.

"Since you going to be in bed all day tomorrow," Jackie said, "we can get started preparing some of the food today." She handed Kathy the beans to snap and some onions to cut up. Jackie prepped the meatloaf and mixed up the slaw.

Michelle was still a child, so inside her apartment, she would play with her dolls. She didn't want any of her schoolmates to know. It was late before she arrived at Jackie's. When she got there, Kathy told her to help.

But Jackie told her to go play with little Lisa.

"That girl doesn't need to be up under grown folks all the time," Jackie said, helping Kathy snap the beans.

Michelle went inside to keep little Lisa company. Lisa was watching cartoons.

Jackie thought this would be a good opportunity to ask Kathy if she'd had "the talk" with Michelle yet. "Have you discussed the bird and bees with Michelle yet?"

"What for?" Kathy replied. "She's just a baby."

"She's a young girl who is around teenagers every day," Jackie replied.

"She's not thinking about boys," Kathy said, "and if I bring it up, she may become curious. So I'm leaving well enough alone."

Jackie leaned over to get more beans to snap.. "You don't have to tell her everything. Just tell her the most important things."

"She doesn't need to know right now," Kathy insisted. "She's still a baby. No guy's going to find my baby desirable with braces on her teeth; her flat chest; her long, loose clothing; her hair in pigtails; and her thick eyeglasses. I have nothing to worry about as long as she looks like this."

"One day, all of that outer layering going to come off," Jackie said. "Don't say I didn't warn you. You keep her too isolated. She needs to mingle with other girls at least sometimes."

"She has nothing in common with these kids," Kathy said. "They're too old for her to be hanging out with."

"Have you ever thought that maybe one day she wants to be a normal teenager?" Jackie dropped another handful of beans into the growing mound in the bowl between her and Kathy.

Kathy frowned. "Look at the kids today. They're pregnant or experimenting with drugs, or they're dropouts or in jail. I don't want my daughter to end up like them. I don't want her to end up here in the projects after she's grown. And I don't want to raise any grandbabies. I don't have the patience you have."

"You know not all these kids are like what you described," Jackie said gently. "Some of them have big dreams, and some of their dreams will come true. Teenage pregnancy, drugs, sex, dropouts—those are all cries for help. They need some attention. I can only do but so much. You see how they respect me and not their own parents. I'm there for them. They always come to me for help. They know they can rely on me to be here for them. Just think—if these kids had parents to rely on, it would solve a lot of problems. Some parents are out partying, drinking, doing drugs and chasing men. That's why kids don't respect their parents. Kids act out intentionally to hurt their parents. It's the only way they know how to get even. They feel that by destroying their own lives, they're hurting their parents. You know what I tell them? 'If you want to get even, become successful. It will make your parents feel guilty because they can't take the credit.'"

"You're right," Kathy agreed. "Tony and I are good parents to Michelle. She's going to turn out just fine. It's too soon to have that talk with her. I'll wait until she's older and develops some."

Kathy stopped talking. She tapped Jackie on the leg to get her attention. "Look, Jackie, look. What a sight."

Jackie raised her head to see what Kathy was trying to get her attention for. They both started laughing as Geraldine and Donnie approached them. With each step Donnie made, he kept pulling up his oversize, baggy pants. The sight of Donnie's long, sandy dreadlocks and his over tan complexion was hilarious to Jackie and Kathy.

When Donnie approached Jackie, he gave her a kiss on the cheek. He gave his pants one good, long, quick jerk up. This almost threw him off balance. He caught himself before it made him look uncool. He decided it's better to keep a hold on his pants with one hand so he wouldn't have another mishap.

Jackie was still checking out the hair. Donnie looked so sweet you couldn't help but love him.

"Is Jamal home?" Donnie asked.

"No, baby, he's at the mall," she told him.

"Is Travis home?"

Still looking and grinning at Donnie's head, Jackie replied, "No, he's at the corner playing ball."

Donnie jumped off the porch—one good, high leap over the porch rail—and jogged while still holding his baggy pants up, heading toward the park.

"Geraldine, why on earth you let that boy mess his hair up like that?" Jackie teased. "It looks like a mop. What do his parents say about his new do?"

Michelle stood in the door listening. She'd heard voices and thought one of them might be Ron's. He hadn't been home since the party.

Kathy and Jackie were still laughing at Donnie's new look. "This boy thinks he's black," Kathy laughed. "He has over baked himself in his mama's tanning booth."

Jackie, laughing uncontrollably added, "I'm surprised his parents haven't fired you. Their only son thinks he's black and only hangs out with poor blacks. Oops, there goes the neighborhood."

"You mean their rich neighborhood." Both women were laughing hysterically now. They couldn't contain themselves.

Michelle interjected, "It's called the urban look."

"He's expressing himself," Geraldine said. "As long as Donnie is happy, his parents are okay."

"Donnie is having an identity crisis," Michelle surmised. "Psychologist Erik Erikson coined this word."

"What?" Jackie said, not laughing anymore. Jackie didn't like kids in grown-up conversations. Every time Michelle talked, she confused Jackie.

"It starts in the teen years when an individual loses a sense of personal sameness and historical continuity," Michelle explained. "Donnie is never around his own ethnic group. He's with us 95 percent of the time. He believes he is a Caucasian Negro—which would be a first." She turned and walked back into the house where Lisa was waiting.

Michelle was too much for Jackie to understand, so Jackie learned to tune her out. Michelle would get explicit when conversing with adults. This was the only time she was superior over her mother.

A taxi pulled up in front of Vera's apartment. Kathy, Geraldine, and Jackie spotted Vera getting out of the cab wearing a blood-colored wig and a revealing, tight-fitting, and very short dress. She liked attention, especially from men.

When Vera saw Jackie and her friends sitting on the porch, she headed toward them. She was puffing on a cigarette and twisting her hips from side to side. Vera was small-framed and pretty. Her heavy makeup took away from her beauty.

As Vera got closer, Jackie said under her breath, "Oh God, what does she want?"

"Hey," Vera called out, drawing the word into three syllables, "what's been going on?" She smirked and added, "every time y'all get together it means you're talking about someone. Who is it now?"

Ignoring Vera's rhetorical question, Jackie interrupted. "Your baby is inside watching TV. You need to go see her. I'm sure she will be happy to finally see you."

"Where is Randy and that sorry no-good ass, Ron? He supposed to be babysitting."

Little Lisa heard Vera's voice. With excitement, she ran to greet her.

Vera bent down to give little Lisa a kiss, and the girl gave her mother a tight hug. "I missed you, mama," she said.

"I missed you too," Vera replied.

"Mama, don't leave us anymore," Lisa pleaded. "I want you to stay home."

"Your bothers can watch you while I'm on my business trips," Vera replied.

"Business trips, pleaseeeee," Jackie said, . More like men trips."

"Stop hating." Vera smiled.

"Randy and Ron are not responsible for your duties," Jackie snapped. "They can't miss school to babysit if Lisa gets sick. Nor should they be worried where there next meal is coming from while you parade around chasing men."

"Mmm, aren't you the testy one," Vera said as she went inside Jackie's apartment in search of something to eat.

When she came back out, she had a plate of food that she was eating.

"What the hell?" said Jackie. "Did you wash your hands?"

"You can cook, girl," said Vera appreciatively. "I haven't had a good home cook meal since I left."

"That is my Sunday dinner you just helped yourself to," Jackie said.

"I know you don't mind. We like family." Vera licked her fingers. "Damn, this is good."

A black Corvette pulled up, and the driver blew its horn.

"Who is that?" Kathy asked.

"This guy I met on the Internet last week," Vera said. "Jackie, since you like babysitting, I need you to babysit again."

"He's nice-looking," Kathy commented.

"You just got back," Jackie said. "You've been gone for four months."

Little Lisa was upset and whining because Vera was leaving again. "Mama, I want to go with you," She pleaded.

"You will," Vera replied.

"Are my brothers coming too?" Lisa asked. "I want Ron with us, Mama. I want my big brother." Lisa start crying. "I want Roooon."

Jackie, making it clear in her tone that she was upset with Vera, broke in. "You need to get somewhere and sit down and raise your kids."

"I'm trying to find a husband for me and a daddy for Lisa," Vera retorted. "I'm getting tired of living in the projects."

"You haven't known this man long enough to be bringing him around your kids," Jackie said, "especially your daughter."

"I know everything I need to know," Vera said sharply. "He lives in South Carolina. He owns his home. He has his own business. And he is ready to get married. We have a lot in common."

Jackie shook her head in disbelief. "You are a desperate, stupid woman," she said.

"I can't believe you said that to me," Vera replied. "You must be a desperate woman too, and stupid for messing with a married man. That's right. I see Gerald creeping over here in the middle of the night while everyone's asleep—and hiding his car at the park so no one can see him creeping on the down low."

Geraldine got up and left in a hurry. "I'll see you later," she called. She didn't like to be around drama; nor did she want to get caught in the middle of it.

Kathy was all ears. This was shocking news, and she wanted to hear more. Kathy couldn't believe her very best friend had not told her she was involved with someone. Gerald was fifteen years younger than Jackie and, as Vera had pointed out, a married man.

"I may be no good in your eyes," Vera continued, "but I'm good enough to want my own husband, not someone else's. You did good, though," she added. "Gerald is fine as hell. I didn't think you had it in you. You got people thinking you're a saint. You know, he came on to me, and I turned him down. I don't want any woman's husband. I want my own. Now I have to be careful with my man around you."

"Get off my porch and go home," Jackie hissed.

"What's wrong?" Vera said. "I strike a nerve? You better be careful; that young boy is a player." Vera was grinning. She knew she'd hit a nerve.

Jackie was tense and upset. "Get off my porch," she demanded.

"We still friends, right," Vera said. "You still gonna watch little Lisa for me."

"You talk too much," Jackie replied.

"How was I to know you didn't tell your friends? You tell them everything about everyone. Why not fill them in on you? You are one part of everyone," Vera said, walking away. "Tell Ron he better not have any of his dirty whores in my apartment."

Little Lisa was crying and begging to go with her mama.

Vera laughed all the way to the car. She hung her head out of the car window to blow Jackie a kiss and started singing the lines of a hit song. "I know what you been doing at night and with whom." She sang loudly so Jackie and anyone else in the vicinity could hear the words of the song clearly.

Little Lisa started to cry again. "I want Ron," she sobbed. "I want my brother."

Michelle came outside to get little Lisa and take her for a walk to calm her down.

Kathy could hardly wait for the kids to get out of hearing range. "Why on earth did you keep this from me?" she demanded. "I'm your best friend. I tell you everything."

"He's married," Jackie replied. "And I'm not comfortable talking about him with anyone, not even with you. I feel guilty as is. You know how this can get in the wrong ears. The less people that know, the better."

"Damn that," Kathy said. "I'm your best friend. If Vera knows, than everyone knows. You know what I want to know."

"Yes," Jackie sighed, drawing out the reply. "He is good. I enjoy the sex."

"Oh yeah!" Kathy said. "I want details. I told you everything about Tony, and he is married." "That's different." Jackie said.

"There's no difference. I want to know how he is in bed. I want details. What's it like being with a younger man? And how big is he?" Kathy was getting overanxious. She could hardly wait for details.

Jackie eventually did share every descriptive detail, from oral sex to how big Gerald was, how long he lasted, and what his favorite position was. Jackie got too comfortable talking about their sex life. She was bragging on how good he was—how he made her scream with pleasure every time they got together.

Jackie wasn't going to admit it to Kathy, but she was falling for Gerald. She prepared home-cooked meals for him. She made sure she was available when he was ready for her. All she thought about was Gerald. She would get jealous when she went to Radio Burger Palace and he would be waiting on young women. She suppressed her feelings. She had to keep reminding herself not to make a fool of herself over a married man. Her motto was, enjoy the sex while it lasts. Once this is over, it may be years before you get some again.

*　*　*

In the months to come, Kathy would enjoy listening to Jackie talk about her and Gerald's sex life. Now that she knew about the pair, Kathy would sometimes look out her window just so she could see when Gerald went over to Jackie's. If Jackie didn't bring it up first, she would.

"I saw Gerald last night going into your apartment," she would say during one such conversation. "He's coming over quite frequently."

"Yeah …," Jackie would reply, her voice drifting off. "He thinks he owns me. You should hear him telling me this stuff. 'I better not catch you with anyone else, or I will kill you.' I catch him sometimes riding by to check up on me."

"Girl!" Kathy would exclaim. "You better be careful. He sounds crazy. When a man talks about killing you, you better take that seriously."

"Oh, he's harmless. He wouldn't hurt a flea. Gerald is so sweet. He's like a kid. He gets jealous, and I kind of like it."

"Well I wouldn't trust any man who threatened to kill me," Kathy would insist. "And I wouldn't stop looking for a single man if I was you. I wouldn't waste my life messing with someone else's husband. You do know he is not going to leave his wife. I can't believe he threatened you, and he's the one messing around. Have you ever given a thought to what he'd do if he does catch you with another man?"

"I told you he's harmless. He has a wife, two small kids, and his own business. He is not gonna harm anyone. He has too much to lose. Besides, he'd just get a replacement."

"Hmmm," Kathy would say slowly. "I wouldn't trust any man who talks about killing."

*　*　*

The weekends went by quickly. On Monday, all the kids were at the bus stop except Ron. It was getting near time for the bus to arrive. Ron was home still in bed, exhausted from a long weekend. Michelle missed seeing him. He was the only man that made her feel special. One day, everyone had jumped in line in front of her and she'd ended up in the back. Ron had never stood in line or had to wait on anything. When he showed up, everyone would say, "Here, Ron, you can get in line" or the driver would say, "Ron, first on the bus." He would just get on the bus and everyone would let him—his brother, Jamal, Donnie, Travis, and Hallie . Ron saw what had happen to Michelle. He picked her up and carried her on the bus, bypassing the ones who cut in line to get ahead of her.

Ron's kindness to Michelle made others give her respect. From that day forward, they never jumped ahead of her again. None of Ron's girlfriends considered Michelle a threat. They knew she wasn't his type.

Although Michelle knew she wasn't Ron's type, it didn't stop her from feeling something for him—something she couldn't explain. Her stomach felt funny whenever he was around, and when he wasn't, her heart felt strange. Her body was telling her she was a woman now. Her mind was telling her she wasn't ready. Michelle didn't understand all these mixed emotions she was getting. She described her feelings in her journal as "the four seasons."

"Winter—I'm so cold longing for your touch. Fall—I'm changing into the woman you want me to be. Spring—I will sprout into maturity. Summer—I will be ready to feel the boldness of your manhood inside of my internal hotness. I want you to be my first and last. I will make you mine," she wrote.

She always looked for Ron. By now, she knew what time he came home and when he didn't. She knew all his girlfriends. She kept all of his goings and comings in her journal. It had been over a week since she'd seen Ron, and it was hurting her to the point that she would cry at night. She knew he was home now. She'd seen him coming in at four o'clock this morning. At the bus stop, everyone was there but Ron.

Michelle said to Jamal, "Ron's going to miss the bus. Someone needs to check on him."

"He'll be all right," Jamal replied. "After his weekend, he needs the rest." Hallie and Jamal laughed.

"If he keeps missing school it will damage his creditability and his chances for getting a football scholarship," Michelle said. "You know every time scouts come to look at Ron, they also take notes on others players on the field."

Jamal needed a scholarship. He had dreams of being a professional football player, marrying Hallie, having a house full of kids, and moving his mom in with them. This was Hallie's dream also—except the kids and Jackie moving in.

Michelle was being manipulative, using Jamal to get Ron. Jamal needed Ron. Ron made him look good on the field.

"Look, baby, I'm going to get Ron's ass out of bed," Jamal said to Hallie. "Look out for Michelle."

"You going to miss the bus fucking with him," Hallie warned.

"We can take the later one," Jamal said. "Here" He handed his books over to her. "Put my books in your locker." He gave her a very long kiss, as if he were going off to war, never to return.

Michelle wanted to go with Jamal, but he convinced her to stay with Hallie.

Hallie gave Michelle a look that said, *You sly devil*. "I know what you just did," she said. "Jamal will never pick up on it. I didn't think you had that in you."

"I have no idea what you're talking about," Michelle insisted.

"All kidding aside, I know who you have a crush on," Hallie said with a sly grin on her face.

Michelle was embarrassed by the knowledge that someone knew her secret. "Please don't tell," she pleaded. "Ron doesn't even know. He would probably laugh at the thought of someone like me having a crush on him. I know I'm not his type."

"Nonsense," Hallie said. "You can be his type, and I can help get him to notice you."

"You can?" Michelle replied. "You would do that for me? But how? He treats me like a kid, and I'm not pretty like those girls he's involved with. Look at me. I'm skinny, tall, flat-chested, and ordinary-looking. I don't even dress stylishly. I wish I were as pretty as you."

"Don't everyone," Hallie smiled. "But that will never happen, sweetheart, You're pretty, Michelle. It's within you. You just have to bring it out. You need to make some major changes."

"Changes?" Michelle asked. "What changes are you referring to?"

"For starters, switch to contacts or ultrathin lenses. Your glasses are like Coca-Cola bottles. When do your braces come off?"

"This year."

"Good," Hallie said. "Start squeezing your breasts every day. That will help them grow. You have long, beautiful hair. At least you have that advantage over some of the girls Ron messes with. They either have weaves or short hair. Your hair almost longer than mine. Long hair turns a man on. You should let it hang loose, especially while having sex. Men love pulling on your hair while making love. Whew! Girl, I'm getting hot just talking about it.

"Let me show you how to let a man know you're interested in him. Keep looking into his eyes. Now watch me. I'm going to pretend you're a guy." Hallie took her cap off, shook her head from side to side, and bent over to let the blood flow to the root of her hair. Then she rose back up slowly and again shook her hair from side to side. She did this again to make sure Michelle got it.

Michelle was watching like she was studying for an examine.

"I hope you got it," Hallie said. "I just gave you your first lesson on how to get a man's attention. Did you see what I just did with my hair? It's called flirting. Only a woman with long hair can use her hair to flirt." She demonstrated to Michelle the hair movement again, to make sure she'd gotten it then added, "You're old enough to do your own hair. You look like a kid with your hair fix like that. That's why Ron treats you like one. You wear your hair like his sister does."

"My mother won't let me wear my hair down," Michelle protested.

"Your mother doesn't want you to look desirable. What you can do is wait till you get to school and put your makeup on and redo your hair. A lot of girls do that. You're not the only one with strict parents. Wash your hair with strawberry shampoo. Men love that scent. They can just eat you up. Remember those barrettes and braids is for kids."

"Those barrettes and *braids are* for kids," Michelle corrected. Michelle hated bad grammar. When she heard someone say a sentence incorrectly, she would simply correct the person by repeating the sentence correctly.

Hallie smiled nonchalantly at Michelle. "Whatever." she said, sounding sarcastic. "Don't do that correction stuff to Ron. Men have problems with women being smarter than them. Ron already has a problem with you being so young and having to tutor him. I wish I was smart as you. Intelligence is a survivor; beauty can be your destruction. My mother keeps telling me that. I don't know what she means. Do you?"

"Maybe she's trying to tell you that beauty will fade away," Michelle suggested. "Your education will stay with you forever."

"Mmmmm, well I'm glad I'm not conceited. Since you like the most popular guy around, you going to have to start putting out. Trust me; Ron isn't hanging with these girls for nothing. Everyone knows you're a virgin, so you better do your homework. And when I say homework, I don't mean school. Men like oral sex. If you don't know what that means, look it up. I get too hot talking about it.

"You know if your parents find out, it's going to be bad for the both of you. Your parents will kill Ron or nail him for statutory rape." Hallie smiled. "You better know what twilight zone you are about to enter, sweetheart. This is a whole different universe you are about to enter. It's for mature women only. Ron is the ruler of his world. Once you enter Ron's world, you will never be able to return to yours. Even if you wanted to, you will never be the same."

"What do you mean by that?" Michelle asked.

"He's a heartbreaker," Hallie said. "All the girls he's been with say he is the best lover they've ever had. You're a virgin with no experience. So be careful. That's all I'm saying."

*   *   *

Jamal arrived at Ron's. Ron didn't want to get up. He kept telling Jamal to go away. Jamal kept nagging him, enough to get him up and dress. They'd already missed the late bus. Ron called one of his female friends with a car to pick them up. She was a college student.

The girl was more than happy to pick Ron up. It meant spending time with him. She felt that, if other girls saw them together, they would think she and Ron were a couple. She offered to buy lunch. Ron was about to refuse, until Jamal tapped him on the shoulder.

"I could go for a burger, fries, and a milkshake," Jamal said.

"Yea, me too," said Ron.

The girl didn't mind spending the money on Ron and his friends. They drove up to Radio Burger Palace and parked the car. She placed the order, and they hung around to chat and eat. Radio Burger was a famous hangout for people of all ages. You could park and eat or cruise your ride and watch music videos.

This was where Jackie had met Gerald. He was the owner. The joint sold every fast food item you could eat. Radio Burger was a great place for Gerald to pick up women. It gave him excuses for coming home late. He had already been with over half the women that came through Radio Burger Palace. Jackie, with her beautiful figure and pretty legs, made him bend over backward. He had to have her. He always waited on her himself. "I got this," he'd tell his employees as he ran to her car. He flirted with her every time he saw her. He was fifteen years younger.

Jackie hadn't been interested at first because he was too young and married. She didn't care how fine he was or how large the imprint she noticed in his jeans. His persuasiveness made her feel desirable. She was curious. It had been years since she'd had a man to touch her. She liked all the attention Gerald gave her. She found herself going to Radio Burger Palace more and more often just to see him.

Gerald wasn't a millionaire, but he lived comfortably. His wife was a stay at home mom. They had a nice home in a nice neighborhood. They wore name brand clothes. He never wanted his wife going anywhere because he didn't want her hearing about his infidelity from her friends or their families. Gerald bragged to others that his wife was a saint—a virgin when they met and a Christian. He trusted her wholeheartedly. She devoted herself to church activities. She practically lived in church. She was very pretty. Sometimes, he would talk about his wife too much to his female women. His wife was also part owner of Radio Burger Palace. He didn't allow her or their two daughters to hang out there..

Gerald's average time frame with a mistress would be less than three months, longer if the sex was good. He would drop them on holidays. He left a trail of broken hearts. Everyone that knew Gerald knew he was no good. He constantly told women he would never leave his wife for them.

Radio Burger Palace was the hosted events that tailored to its theme and clientele—car shows for special model vehicles like Corvettes and Escalades and motorcycles clubs rallies just to name a few }People would cruise through just to show off their clean, shiny rides.

When Gerald saw Ron and Jamal, he came over to the car and leaned in the window to talk to Jamal. "Why you're not in school? Does your mom know you hooking?"

"We're on the way back," Jamal said. "We're on our lunch break." This was the first time Jamal had to lie or explain himself to anyone other than Hallie. If his mother knew he wasn't at school, she would be furious. His other concern was Hallie. She didn't want him to waste his time on Ron all day, and he'd already spent over half of it with him. Now he was going to have to listen to Hallie rant and rave the rest of the day.

Gerald asked Jamal, "How your mother doing?"

"She all right," Jamal replied.

"Did she work today?"

"Yeah."

Gerald left to serve other customers.

"What that nigga asking about your mom for?" Ron asked.

"I don't know, man," Jamal replied.

They were both puzzled about Gerald having asked about Jackie. "You know he has a reputation," Ron said. "He's just about screwed every woman in town."

"I know man. I better not catch that motherfucker hanging around my house. Every time I come here, he's asking about my mom. He's always giving us a hookup whenever we come here."   "Yeah … What's up with that?"

"You know he's married with two little girls," Ron's girl interjected. "Everyone knows his reputation. He chases after every female he sees. He even hit on me." She said this last bit hoping to get a reaction from Ron.

"We shouldn't even go to school today," Ron said. "We already missed over half the day."

"Nah," Jamal protested. "Hallie's already going to be pissed. I have to come up with some excuse."

"Forget that witch. You need to be more concerned about your mother. You're more concerned about Hallie than your mom. What's up with that? Stop being a wimp, man."

"Don't say that. I stand up to Hallie."

"You will stand up to your mama before you stand up to Hallie," Ron argued. "You know that's not right, man. Hallie really got you by the balls, and everyone knows it."

Jamal looked disturbed. He got quiet and then said after a while, "So this is what you and the rest of my friends think." Jamal didn't say another word during the ride to school.

Once they arrived at school Ron and Jamal went their separate ways without saying a word.

When they got mad at each other it didn't last long. After school, Jamal had had enough time to cool off. He knew Ron was right. Being told the truth had hit a nerve. Ron knew not to rub it in. He and Jamal never stayed mad at each other for too long. Their friendship outweighed any obstacle that got in the way. Not even Hallie could pull them apart, but she continued to try.

The school bell rang, signaling the end of another school day. Students rushed to get to their destinations.

Deena asked Michelle if she was staying after school.

"No, I have to get home," Michelle said.

"Oh, that's right; you're tutoring Ron," Hallie said. "If you like, I'll show you how to apply makeup just enough so that your mother won't even notice."

"I would like that."

"So where is this tutoring taking place?"

"At home."

Hallie broke out laughing. "I don't even have to guess. Your mother will be in the same room while you're tutoring. I couldn't live like that. You need to start standing up for yourself. Make her stop treating you like a baby."

Michelle glanced at the clock on the wall behind Hallie. "Well, I need to go before the bus leaves," she said softly.

Hallie yelled after Michelle, "Don't do anything I wouldn't." Then she muttered to herself, "Oh hell, why did I even bother saying that to you. Nothing's going to happen anyway."

Deena overheard, and they both start laughing.

"I thought Ron didn't want her to tutoring him," Deena said.

"His coach gave him an ultimatum," Hallie explained.

"They have a game today. Is he going to be able to play?" Deena asked.

"Yeah, he's playing. He wouldn't miss a game. I doubt he'll even show up to be tutored. If so, it will be late, and Michelle's mother is not going for that. The girl is in bed by nine."

"Damn, if I had parents like that, I would run away from home." reply Deena

Michelle was already on the bus. She was excited. She rushed home to get everything in order for Ron's arrival. She made sure the house was clean and smelled good. She took her hair down and applied Vaseline on her lips for a shine. Kathy helped Michelle make some snacks for her guest. Afterward, Michelle tried to get her mother to go over Jackie's.

Kathy refused. "I'm not leaving you alone with a boy."

"Mom!" Michelle protested. "Why don't you trust me to be alone with a guy? What's the worst that could happen?"

"Ron is way older than you and likes to play around."

"Well there be no playing around here; you can trust me. Ron looks at and treats me like a kid," she said, disappointment etched in her voice.

"You I trust; Ron I don't."

Michelle was frustrated. She remembered Hallie telling her she needed to stand up to her mother. "My God, mother, stop treating me like a child!" she said. "You don't even trust me to be alone to study with a guy. You're the strictest parent on earth. I hate how you treat me."

Kathy looked at her daughter in surprise. "Michelle, what's gotten into you? You have never talked to me like this!"

Michelle was crying now. "I want some breathing room," she choked out. "You are suffocating me. I might as well go stay with my daddy and his wife."

"Okay, let's calm down," Kathy said. "What do you want, Michelle?"

Michelle took a deep breath. "Well, number one, I want to wear contacts. Two, I want to wear makeup. Three, I want to be able to hang out with some of my friends. And four, I want to go on dates."

"Two, three, and four are out," Kathy replied. "No way. That's not going to happen. I will consider contacts and a little lip gloss. And that's it. There will be no boys hanging around here. You are too young. You can ask me again when you're eighteen."

Michelle knew she was not going to win this debate.

Ron was two hours late. Kathy helped Michelle serve the snacks, which he didn't touch. Ron was well mannered and soft-spoken. He apologized for being late. He gave a smile and shook Kathy's hand. Even Kathy was hypnotized by his charm. She found herself daydreaming about him. She had to snap herself out of it. Kathy said silently to herself, *Damn he fine. If I knew it wasn't against the law, whew!* Kathy was staring Ron up and down and oozing at the sight of him. *Get a hold of yourself. This boy is up to something. All these college women he sees. Why can't one of them tutor him?*

While Michelle went to get her books, Kathy took the time to warn Ron. "Ron, I want to say this to you. Michelle is a baby—my baby. At fourteen, she's the smartest and the youngest to be accepted to Yale. She already wrote a summary in *Time Medical Journal*. We have great expectations for her. Her father and I are not about to let anyone ruin her life or her future. If you're trying to use my daughter for your personal sexual needs, then you better think again. Her father will kill anyone who messes Michelle's life up."

Ron was dumbfounded. He thought he was there to be tutored, not to hear a speech. He had no idea what Kathy was talking about and why she was saying all this.

"This is a warning just in case you try something with my daughter," Kathy finished.

Michelle walked in on the speech. She was embarrassed.

Ron wasn't scared and didn't pay much attention to Kathy's threats. If Kathy only knew what Ron thought about Michelle, she could have saved her speech. Ron didn't find Michelle appealing at all. Ron wanted to get out of there ASAP after that speech of Kathy's. He had to find an excuse to leave. He pretended his cell phone beeped with a text message. He jumped up and told Michelle that something had come up, and he had to go.

"We haven't even started yet," Michelle protested. "Can it wait? What could be more important?

"No!" Ron said. "I have to go."

"You're going to fail if I …"

"Yeah, we can do this some other time," Ron interrupted. "I really have to go." Ron walked out quickly. Once outside, he took a deep breath.

He called Jamal and told him about what had happened. "Man, this girl's mama is crazy. She's tripping. She's rambling on like I want her daughter."

"Say what! Did you stick around?"

"Heck no, I got the hell out of there fast. And no, before you ask, I'm not going back."

"What you going to do about the coach? You know what he said."

"I don't care. I am not up to being lectured or threaten by parents of a girl I have no desire for. Where in the hell did she get this idea that I'm interested in her daughter?"

Michelle was furious with her mother for butting in her life as usual. "Why would you say that to him?" she demanded.

"I'm protecting you," Kathy said. "I know about Ron's reputation. He is a smooth operator."

"I also know about his reputation," Michelle snapped. "You seem to have failed to remember that he was here to get tutored while you sat in the same room with us. What's the worst that could happen with the three of us?" She stormed off to her bedroom and slammed the door.

Kathy followed her and yelled through the locked door. "How dare you raise your voice to me? I'm still your mother. And don't slam that door again!"

Kathy was in disbelief. She called Jackie to share what had just happened between her and Michelle. Jackie invited Kathy to come over and sit on the front porch with her.

"I don't know what's gotten into Michelle lately. She don't want to spend the summer with her dad anymore. She's putting on my makeup, wearing perfume, and wearing her hair down. She wants me to take her to get contacts."

"She's growing up," Jackie said, "and she's becoming interested in boys. You know it's time for this to happen. I told you to have the talk with her."

"No, it's not that. It's the pressure of school. She's so much younger then everyone there. I may have to pull her out and put her back in private school."

"Stop treating her like a child," Jackie said gently. "Meet her halfway. Get her some contacts and let her wear her hair down if that's what she wants. She's probably becoming self-conscious about her appearance. Some kids could be picking on her, and the kids in private school are no different. Michelle didn't like it at that private school. If you force her to go back, you may lose all control of her. Try to meet her at least halfway."

While they were talking, a black SUV with tinted windows was driving by slowly, with music playing very loudly.

Someone yelled, "It's a drive-by!"

Parents ran around grabbing their kids and taking them inside for safety.

A back tinted window of the SUV rolled down long enough for someone to throw a cigarette butt out.

It was enough for Jackie to get a glimpse inside and to recognize two of the backseat passengers. "It's Lee and Sean!" Jackie yelled. "They know better than that. They're scaring everyone." Jackie jumped up from her porch and walked toward the SUV. She was yelling for the SUV to stop.

When Sean and Lee saw that it was Jackie, they told the driver, Snake to go. "Let's get the hell away from here," Lee said. "It's Miss Jackie."

"Damn!" Sean added. "I knew we shouldn't have come on this side of town."

"Speed up, man," Lee said. "We don't want her catching us."

Kathy was yelling at Jackie. "Are you crazy, Jackie? You don't know who's in that SUV. Come back."

As the SUV sped a little faster, Jackie picked up the pace too. She was running behind the SUV.

"Damn!" said Sean.

"What y'all tripping for?" Snake laughed, watching Sean and Lee trying to get the smell of reefer out of the SUV and their clothes. "You ought to see yourselves acting like mama's boys. I thought y'all was gangsterfied.

You ought to call yourselves baby gang." Snake grinned and laughed at his joke. "Who's this Miss Jackie that y'all up in arms about?" He was still laughing.

"Miss Jackie is Jamal and Travis's mother," Lee explained. She's the woman that has all the cookouts for us—you know, the one we were telling you about."

Snake watched Jackie in his rearview mirror. Snake pulled over and stopped. He kept staring at her.

Lee and Sean said in union, "What the hell you pull over for?"

"Keep driving," Sean added. They were panicking. It was hard to get the odor out, even with all the windows down. They sprayed incense spray on themselves and inside the SUV.

"Damn!" Snake said. "Miss Jackie is fine as hell. Look at that body. She's finer than some of these young ass girls. Those girls have nothing on Miss Jackie. She's got some pretty sexy legs. I can imagine what she's like in bed. She's hot. Oh man, I got to hook up with her."

"Are you crazy?!" Lee said. "Keep dreaming, man. We all live on wishful thinking, but we got enough sense to know better. You or any men don't stand a chance. You have to go through her sons, Jamal and Travis and their best friends, Ron and Randy. They all are overprotective of her."

"Did you say Ron," Snake asked, "the all-star player, Ron—thee Ron?"

"Yeah, man," Lee said. "That's the Ron I'm referring to."

"Oh, man, he's my idol," Snake said. "I got to meet him." As Jackie was getting closer, Snake was rushing to erase the smell from his clothes. He began spraying car incense on himself and inside, and he put some chewing gum in his mouth.

"Yeah, we hang out with Ron," Lee said. "We're on the same football team. And we sometimes shoot hoops together. You ought to come to some of the games."

Snake wasn't listening. He was trying to groom himself. "He's going pro. I know it," Snake said, getting back in the conversation. "He's the greatest I've seen on the field since …" Suddenly he stopped. "Hello, Mrs. Robinson," he breathed.

When Jackie approached the SUV, Snake jumped out, smile, and said accidently, "Hello, Mrs. Robinson."

Lee and Sean laughed loudly.

Jackie didn't catch on. She asked "Why are you driving around here like you're about to do a drive-by. You're scaring everyone in the neighborhood."

They all looked humble and said they weren't doing a drive-by. "We were just cruising and looking for our boys so we can get a game started, Miss Jackie," Lee explained.

Snake tried to make himself look good by saying. "I told Sean and Lee we should just park and walk around. They insisted on cruising."

"The music was blasting too loud, and I can smell drugs," Jackie replied.

Snake tried again to make himself look better by throwing the blame on his friends. "Miss Jackie, my father got me this SUV. I told Sean and Lee not to smoke that stuff in it. It's gonna be hard to get the smell out of my ride."

Lee and Sean gave each other a look of surprise. "Who is he trying to impress?" Sean said.

"That nigga wasting his time," Lee agreed. "She ain't falling for that."

"Don't do it again," Jackie said. "Seriously, that dope will fry your brain. I don't want y'all scaring the neighborhood again. That goes for you too, Snake."

"Yes, ma'am," they all said together.

Snake was a small-time drug dealer. His mother was on crack. He never met his father. He dropped out of school during eighth grade. He was illiterate. No one had the patience to teach him how to read. The teachers didn't have patience with the students who couldn't keep up. They only taught the ones who could keep up. Snake couldn't keep up. Snake dropped out and sold drugs just to feed and clothe himself and his seven siblings. He was too young to get a legal job. His biggest problem was his mother. She would steal his dope and money. When he bought groceries for his siblings, his mother would sell it.

Snake had some clients that worked at Fast Burger World. He struck a deal with them. If they let his siblings come every day to eat, in return he would give them some drugs to cover the cost of the food.

Jackie didn't know about Snake's drug dealings. Snake would find out about Jackie's compassionate heart, as he and his sibling would soon be her added family. It was no secret that Jackie would do anything to help others in need. She had fed, clothed, and helped over half the people in the projects.

Jackie decided to walk back home. Snake threw the SUV keys to Lee. He wanted to walk with Jackie. She invited them back to her place for hot dogs and burgers.

"How are your grades in school?" Jackie asked Snake. "You are still in school, aren't you?"

"I had to drop out so I could take care of my brothers and sisters," Snake said.

"Where is your mother? Why she can't take care of them? You need your education."

"My mom, if you can call her that, is strung out on crack. I'm the sole provider for my family."

"Oh, honey, that's a shame," Jackie said sincerely. "You shouldn't have to drop out of school. This is too much of a responsibility for you. You're still a child."

"Miss Jackie, I would like to go back to school," Snake said. "I dropped out because school was too hard. The teachers go too fast for me. I couldn't keep up."

"What are you having problems in?" Jackie asked.

Embarrassed to say that he was having problems in everything, Snake squirmed. "I, um, I have problems reading."

"I'll make a deal with you," Jackie offered. "Have your brothers and sisters come here to eat and take your mother a plate also. We can't let her starve."

"You want me to pay you?" Snake asked.

"No."

"Then what's the deal?"

"You come here and let me teach you how to read and write. Then I want you to enroll back in school. Is that a deal?"

Snake wasn't sure. "Miss Jackie, it takes me longer to learn. No one has the patience with me."

Jackie raised her eyebrows. "Is this a deal or not?"

"I don't know, Miss Jackie," Snake said. "It's just a waste of time. My life is useless."

"Never ever say that about yourself," Jackie replied, her voice strong. "If I have you reading in three months, will you at least get your GED? You can always go back later for college or trade school. Then you can get a legal job and get custody of your siblings. Now, do we have a deal?"

"Okay, I'll try it for a month."

"Oh, just a reminder," Jackie added. "Don't come around me smelling like reefer. I don't like the smell of it."

They were all having a good time eating, laughing, telling jokes, and playing cards when Jamal, Donnie, Ron, Travis, and Randy showed up. Once they arrived, the gathering turned into a party. The excitement was overwhelming. For once, Snake forgot about his problems. He was surrounded with good people who reminded him what an adolescent's life should be like. He was having a good time. He knew about Ron, Donnie, and Jamal's reputations. Just being around them could help his image.

Snake always dated older women, women old enough to be his mother. They didn't have class; nor were they sophisticated or pretty. Older women were desperate for a nice young man. They were easy to get and bed down. They loved supporting their man with clothes and jewelry. They loved to cook home-cooked meals for him. He got the motherly attention from his women friends that he'd never gotten from his mother.

Since Jackie was teaching Snake how to read, he started hanging out with Jamal and Ron. He went to all the games and hung out with them. He did not sell or carry drugs on him when he was around Ron and Jamal. Soon Snake was considered popular. He even started dating one of Hallie's best friends, Deena.

Deena's parents were well-to-do. She was spoiled. The only girl in the family, she had a younger brother. This was the first time Snake had dated a young and beautiful girl. Since he only been with older women, Snake was over-experienced. He thought Deena would be mature. He had to teach her how to make love. He found out she was too needy and cried all the time when she got mad at him. She was nothing but trouble—calling all the time, arguing over stupid stuff. If he look at a woman, she went into a jealous rage.

Deena couldn't handle Snake's experience. It blew her mind. Snake knew he was a great lover. After all, he'd learned how to satisfied women from his older women. He had hoped Jackie would become one of them. But it had never happened. She treated Snake like he was one of her sons. He eventually gave up the ideal of sex with her and thought only of her as a mother figure.

Snake spread himself around to other young girls, and Deena would run them off. He had to walk on thin ice with Deena. She knew about his dealings with drugs. When it came to getting caught cheating, he'd never had to explain himself before. But now it was different. Deena had his hands tied, and he didn't like it. She was always following him. If she saw his car parked outside one of his females friend's house, she would bust his car windows or threaten to call the police and report that he was selling drugs, which he didn't need.

Hallie wanted to know why her friend was acting so crazy. Deena told her Snake had a big dick and could screw his ass off. He made her come four or five times in a session. Sometimes he could screw all night long. She had to beg him to stop. He was the best she'd ever had. He blew her mind. She couldn't stop wanting to be around him all the time. She was always complaining to her friends about him cheating, about him not answering his phones or not being at home.

Snake tried to break it off (although he had never considered himself officially going out with her). She told him that if he broke up with her, she was going to the cops and telling them where his stash was. He found himself hating her. She was always threatening to call the cops when things didn't go her way. When he stopped having sex with her, she lost her mind. She was nothing but trouble to him.

Deena's parents and friends noticed that she had changed when she'd gotten involved with Snake. She skipped school. She turned on her parents and friends. She didn't care about her appearance. She didn't act—nor look—sophisticated anymore. She was getting in fights over Snake.

She would bang on all of the motel's room doors if she thought Snake was there, yelling "I know you in there with one of your old, ugly bitches. I'm not leaving until you come out."

Snake wouldn't come out until she started breaking his car windows.

One night, Snake finally snapped. He'd had enough. He grabbed her by her arm and jerked her. "Damn dumbass bitch. You paying for my car windows."

"What the hell you doing here?" Deena demanded. "You told me you were going to drop a bag off and you would be right back."

Snake grabbed Deena by the arm. "I don't need to explain myself to you."

Deena's voice rose. She wanted the other woman to hear. "You didn't say that this morning when you were screwing me."

The older woman was standing in her front door said. "Snake, get your shit and leave, and don't call me anymore."

Snake turned toward the older woman. "What's wrong with you?"

"I don't play with kids," she replied, "and this shit is childish. Your little girlfriend is crazy. I don't have time for drama."

Deena was ready to fight. "Bitch, you messing with my man. You're old. You ain't got nothing on me."

"Shut up!" Snake yelled, trying unsuccessfully to drown out Deena's attempts to fight with the older woman.]

Still in the doorway, the older woman's eyes narrowed. "You better contain ghetto child before I bust a cap in her stupid ass."

Deena made a move toward the older woman. "You not going to do nothing," she taunted. "You're just jealous because I'm young and prettier. I will kick your …"

Snake cut in, stopping Deena from moving any closer. "Didn't I tell you to shut the hell up?" "Get in the car before I knock the hell out of you."

Deena raise her voice louder as Snake rush her away from the house.

"Damn!" He jerked her arm and shoved her in the car.

After Deena was in the car, Snake went back to patch things up with the older woman. He really liked her. But she wouldn't give in.

"Look," Snake said. "I'm going to drop this crazy bitch off. I'll be back."

"Snake, it's over. Don't come back. I mean it." She threw what little clothes he had out and slammed the door, leaving him outside begging.

Deena, sitting in the car, listened to everything. She was hurt and crying.

Snake returned to the car even more pissed. "You gonna stop fucking my life up," he told her. "I have told you we don't go together. What part of 'we don't go together' don't you understand?"

"I love you," Deena cried. "That old woman can't do anything for you. She's old and ugly. I'm young and pretty. Look at me. A lot of men want me, but I choose you. I love you so much. I will do anything for you. I will. Just tell me how to make you love me. But don't ask me to stop loving you because I can't. It will hurt me too much. I will kill myself. If you leave me, I will," she sobbed.

Snake felt sorry for her. He took her home—which was to his place, as she was now living with him and his family. He made love to her all night long. He introduced her to her first drug. He kept her stoned. This was his payback for running off his women.

Deena would continue chasing off Snake's girlfriends, and he would continue cheating. She would miscarry twice. Snake would get another girl pregnant and still maintain a relationship with two women. Deena would be stuck taking care of his siblings and two of his outside babies. Deena had dropped out of school. She no longer hung out with Hallie or any of the girls in the "pretty girls' group." Her parents got tired of her disobedience and her drugs and alcohol use.

Hallie never used drugs. She believed drug use would destroy your beauty.

Deena was living in the poorest, most drug infested side of town in a small two bedroom house. She loved Snake so much that she gave up everything. Since she couldn't stop him from cheating, she accepted it. She got tired of hearing him tell her, "You don't own me. I don't want you." She continued telling him how much she loved him and would show him how much.

Snake would split his time between Deena and his other women. It drove Deena crazy when he didn't have sex with her for a while. When he came home, she would be all over him, kissing and licking him all over and begging. "Please, I need you. I need to feel you inside me now," she would beg, slipping one hand inside his pants to caress what was growing bigger. She was at a point of begging or doing whatever it took to get him to make love to her. She was desperate to feel his hardness inside her. It had been weeks since he'd last touched her. She would caress, kiss, and suck him until they both were satisfied.

From all the moaning and screaming Deena did while he was having sex with her, Snake knew she was weak and wasn't going anywhere. That's why he cheated and did it in her face. As long as she was high, she stayed calm.

Snake was no longer hanging around with Ron and Jamal. Once Jackie had helped him get his GED, he'd stop coming around. He didn't want a nine-to-five job. He wanted to be his own boss.

Deena's parents tried everything to get her away from Snake. They sent her away to stay with an aunt in California. She just ran away to get back to Snake. It crushed them to see her turn out like this. She wouldn't listen to anyone. She became difficult. She got in fights with her parents.

Once, she drew a knife on her brother. That was the last straw for her parents. They told her to get out.. She had become too much for them to bear. Her staying away was for the best until she got herself together—which she never did.

Chapter Eleven

Donnie's Birthday

Donnie sixteenth birthday was a huge event for his parents and grandparents. He got a twenty-five thousand-dollar credit card and a black Escalade. Whatever Donnie wanted, between his parents and grandparents, he got it.

Donnie never asked for much. For his birthday, he wanted a black, tinted Escalade. He didn't just want it for him; he wanted the Escalade for his friends too. The Escalade was off the showroom floor. He made sure the sound system was hooked up the way he wanted it. He got all the latest sounds.

His parents were planning a family birthday party, which Donnie didn't want. The family party always turned out to be his parents' and grandparents' party. Donnie's friends could not come to the family party. So this kind of party was boring. He would get his gifts and listen to them dictate his future. They would get drunk, and he would leave with Geraldine.

Once his family had left for London, Donnie would have Geraldine arrange a party so he could invite his friends. He got the Escalade from his parents. His grandparents gave him the credit card. And Geraldine gave him a bottle of cologne by his favorite rap singer. He couldn't wait to show off his new ride.

His parents and grandparents felt that this was the best time to bring up the subject of his future again—what college he should attend and what major he would take. Donnie didn't share the same future plans as his parents and grandparents. He was living for today and having lots of fun doing so. Since they'd brought it up again, he broke the news about what he was going to do. And they were not ready to hear it. He had decided to attend the same college Ron and Jamal were going to, rather than his parents' alma mater. He also told his parents that he was going to marry Nikkie, his African American girlfriend, and become a famous rapper.

When he told his parents this, they laughed. They didn't take any of it seriously.

His grandfather, on the other hand, was livid. "He can't be serious," Donnie's grandfather exclaimed. "I told you to put the boy in military school. Now look at him. He's talking about being a … what—what the hell is a rapper? What does a rapper do?"

"Granddad, it's flowing, spitting words to music," Donnie explained, after saying that he then left.

"What a waste," his grandfather said, shaking his head.

Donnie's mother cut in. "The therapist said he will grow out of this notion once he graduates."

"I sure hope so," Donnie's grandfather said, still in a huff. "Military school will teach him some discipline. We can still put him in one. He's hanging around too many blacks. Look at how the boy dressed. His pants are so big you can see the crack of his ass. And what's wrong with his hair?"

"It's the latest style," Donnie's mother said.

"That's bullshit!" his grandfather exclaimed as he fixed himself another scotch and whiskey. "You tell me you can't dress your son."

"We teach him to make his own decisions," she replied. "He is young and impressionable. He will grow out of this phase."

"He will grow out of it when you put him in a private school with his own kind. I'll bet you that he spends that money we gave him on those friends of his. They are going to use him, you know that."

"You are prejudiced," Donnie's mother countered, "a damn racist to the heart. His friends are good kids."

Donnie's grandmother broke in. "That's enough!" she declared. "What Donnie does with his money is none of our business."

"Why not?" her husband demanded. "It should be our business. He's the only heir we have. We need to know what he does with his money now. It will tell us how he will handle it in the future. I have every right to make his business my business." He fixed himself yet another drink.

"Dad, don't you think you've had enough to drink," Donnie's father said.

"Let your father be," Donnie's grandmother replied. "He has a lot on his mind. The doctor told him drinking is good for his heart."

"That explains the high percentage of alcoholics," Donnie's mother said, fixing herself another martini.

"Honey, please don't get them started," Donnie's father chided.

"Me?" she protested. "Get them started? You're always taking your parents side. Your father started four drinks ago."

"You should have had more kids," Donnie's grandfather said. "At least one of them would have taken after my side of the family. I told you, son, to get that pretty little secretary of yours pregnant."

"You told him what?!" Donnie's mother exploded in anger. "How dare you?! What's wrong with your sperm count? You only have one child."

Donnie's father grabbed his wife by the arm. "Let's go to bed," he said. "You've said enough." He was trying to put the flame out before the fire got out of control. They had all had too much to drink.

"For your information, we think the world of my son," Donnie's grandmother said. "He is a very intelligent young man."

"He's not that intelligent," grandfather shot out. "Look what the hell he married—a gold digger." Donnie's grandfather took another sip of his drink.

"How dare you!" Donnie's mother turned to her husband. "Are you going to let him keep talking to me like that?"

Donnie's father turned to his father. "Dad, every time you come here you pick a fight with my wife. Mom, please take Dad to bed. He's had enough to drink."

"How can you let him get away with talking to me like that? He's in my home!" Donnie's mother pointed to herself. "This is my home!" she sobbed, rocking unsteadily on her feet.

"Correction," her father-in-law said cruelly, "this my home. I brought this house for my son and a wife who could produce heirs—lots of them. This mansion was a waste on a family of three. My grandson doesn't know what race he is."

"Dad, please give it a rest," Donnie's father begged.

"Well, its true dear," his mother said, defending her husband. "Donnie thinks he's black." The word *black* was spoken in a whisper. "We don't have a problem with black people," she added.

Granddad broke in, "Hell, I can't tell what's what anymore. Donnie's beginning to look black. Look at him. The boy has darkened his skin. People just aren't satisfied to be who they are. Blacks want to be white, and whites want to be black."

"Would you love him any less if he were black?" Donnie's father asked. "Or is your money meant for whites only?" He took his sobbing, drunken wife to the bedroom, leaving his intoxicated father with something to think about.

"You know, he has a point," Donnie's grandmother said when she was alone with her husband. "Would you love Donnie any less? I don't know about you, but he is our only grandson, and I don't believe we're going to get anymore. Donnie's going through a phase. He'll grow out of it sooner or later. He could color himself blue and I will love him the same."

"My will won't change," her husband replied. "I wouldn't change it if he decided to wake up tomorrow and become a queer. I wouldn't like it. But he—or whatever the hell he is when he turns twenty-one—will be worth over seventy million dollars or he'll be a billionaire. I wish I could be around to see how he'll use it."

"I know, dear, me too." She patted her husband and rubbed his back as he sit on the edge of the bed, his head leaning on her stomach. "You're going to be looking from the heavens. We both will. We will be so proud of him. He's going to be somebody important."

Donnie's granddad sobbed suddenly. "You think God is going to forgive me?" he asked his wife. "I've done a lot of bad things. Our grandson can't ever know. You have to promise me he will never find out the things I've done or the organizations I've been involved with. I need you to promise me. There's one thing I have to tell you."

"I thought we did all our confessions when you found out your cancer was back," his wife replied gently. "Have you changed your mind about telling your son?"

"He doesn't need to know," he snapped. "His gold digging wife will be counting the money before I'm dead." He grabbed her by the hands and buried his head in her chest, sobbing. "There's something I've kept hidden from you. You have to promise me you won't leave me now. I need you and your forgiveness. I want to apologize. All these years, I've been living a lie. I had an affair many years ago."

"I know about your affairs."

"This one was different. It wasn't just any affair. She was a young woman I met going back and forth on my business trips. The relationship lasted three years."

"Why tell me this now?" his wife asked. "What's so different about this affair from the others?"

"She was African American, and she was pregnant with my child." He dropped his head in shame.

"I thought your organization disliked blacks," she said, anger creeping into her voice. "Or was that just a cover-up?"

"I was curious. She was so breathtaking. I—I couldn't resist. Not that she was any better than you. You have to understand. I was young and so full of myself back then. I couldn't help myself."

"Stop it!" his wife exclaimed. "I don't want to hear anymore. It's the past. It is the past, isn't it?"

"Well sort of. I mean I haven't been unfaithful since. I've been trying to make things right. I'm so sorry for putting you through this. Please forgive me."

Tears rolled down his wife's face. "Where is the child?"

"I don't know. She disappeared when I threatened to kill them if she had the baby." He used a low tone when he spoke the word *kill*. "We argued. She said no to an abortion. Then she left town before I got to her. I haven't seen her since."

"A baby," she whispered, getting choked up. "We lost our daughter and you went off and had a baby by another woman. Then you threatened to kill them. What kind of man did I marry? Have you even tried to find them?"

"I tried once a long time ago," he confessed. "I didn't have much luck. I guess I didn't put much effort into finding them. I was afraid you'd find out and leave me. This is where I need you. I want to leave them in my will—twenty-five million if they're found. If not, it will go to the Negro

College Fund. I have to do right. I have to make things right. This is where I need you. If I don't find them before I die, please, I want you to continue searching. Please, promise me you won't stop until you find them. Make sure they get the money. Please," he sobbed. "Please"

"Money won't make up for time lost," his wife replied. "Did she know you were married?"

"Let's not go there not now at least," her husband said, regaining his composure. "This is my fault, not hers. I understand that you hate me right now. But I need you more now than ever. Don't take your hate out on her. You're too good for that. That's why I fell in love with you. You were different. Please don't change now—not now. I feel like God is punishing me. Nothing has gone right in this family. We lost our daughter, my son married a gold digger, my grandson doesn't know what race he is, and I have a child out there somewhere. I may never get to see her or him. God, please let me see my child before I die."

In the next bedroom, Donnie's mother was trying to reason with her husband. "Is there any way your parents can stop coming here? Their visits are tearing our family apart. Your father gets drunk and starts fights with me."

"Maybe if you stop feeding him alcohol and drinking it yourself, you all will be sober enough to get along." Donnie's father turned off the bedside lamp on his side. He turned over, facing away from his wife.

"You're a real ass, just like your father," she said.

"Cut the crap. I'd like to sleep instead of fighting with you tonight. By the way, my father, the ass, is the one with the money that's keeping you up with that over-the-top lifestyle you're so used to. So you might want to kiss his ass a lot instead of criticizing it. Cut the light off."

She cut the light off and turned her back to him. "How dare you talk to me like that? I could divorce you and take this house and half your money."

"Don't count your cash yet. If my father ever found out you were pregnant twice and aborted them, I can only hope he'd go easy on you. You don't know what that man is capable of. I only keep you around so Donnie can have a picture-perfect family. Our marriage was over after the first abortion. Our marriage was based on you giving me kids. It's in the contract my father had you to sign. Or did you even bother reading it before you signed it? Let me guess, you were too busy counting my millions. I can call the old man in here and tell him you killed two of his heirs."

"Go to hell."

Remaining with their backs turned to each other, they both fell asleep.

*   *   *

Geraldine left the family party as soon as the drinking began. Donnie knew how skittish Geraldine could get when she was around drinking, so he took her for a ride in his new Escalade.

Donnie loved his grandfather, even though the old man was prejudiced. When he got lump sums of money from his grandparents, he made sure he spent it all on his black friends. He also liked playing jokes on his grandfather.

Donnie would tell his friends how his granddad was, and they'd all get a good laugh from some of the stories. Donnie's grandfather was like the Archie Bunker of their generations but even funnier.

Once, he took Hallie to his grandparents' house, just to get his grandfather stirred up. He decided to play a trick on his granddad. Donnie pretended he and Hallie had gotten married and that she was with child. Hallie had a dark tan and a fake pregnant pillow. She wore a dreadlocked wig, and Donnie talked about dropping out of high school and becoming a rapper. He even rapped for his grandparents. He didn't hold back on the cussing or refrain from using the words *killing*, *bitches*, and *whores*. Donnie and Hallie had carried on so much that his granddad had ended up having to go to the emergency room. He was released the next day.

Donnie's mother couldn't stop laughing when Donnie told her what he and Hallie had done. It wasn't the first time Donnie had played a trick on his granddad.

Since Donnie was their only grandchild, his grandparents tolerated his tricks and games. They didn't care what Donnie did. They may not like his actions, but he was still the only heir. His granddad was leaving the bulk of his estates, trust, and money to Donnie when they died.

Donnie's mother knew this. She was not going to upset the person who would be in charge of writing out her checks. She told nannies, cooks, housekeepers, or anyone who worked for the family to make sure Donnie got whatever he wanted and needed. The hired help hardly ever saw Donnie, and when they did, they thought he was Geraldine's son.

Donnie's mother was not the hands-on type. That's why she'd only had one child. Donnie's granddad had wanted more grandkids and resented Donnie's mother for not having them. That's why, when they all came together, the gathering usually ended with the same argument. The argument would follow a predictable pattern. The evening would be going smoothly, everyone happy to see each other. Then the drinking would begin. Granddad would always be the first to turn a perfect evening into a disaster. The peacemaker was Donnie's father, and Donnie's grandmother who stayed out of the arguments but came to her husband's defense when something was said to her disliking.

When Donnie and Geraldine arrived back at the mansion, they noticed the quietness and turn in too. Donnie was too excited to sleep. He was in the garage all night wiping down his new ride. His family found him early the next morning sleeping in his Escalade.

They had a family breakfast and started making plans for the next family get-together. They acted as if they had already forgotten about the argument from the day before.

Donnie couldn't wait to show off his new ride to his friends. He left home earlier than usual. He drove up in front of Jamal and Travis's apartment and parked. Music was banging from the stereo. The girls that were hanging around admired the ride and tried to get Donnie to give them a ride. They were touching everything. This was too much for Donnie. "Don't slam my door like that," he said. "Leave the music alone. Don't be adjusting my seats like that. Man! Y'all act like you never been around a new ride before."

One girl jumped on top of the Escalade to sit. "What the hell!" Donnie exclaimed. "Girl, are you crazy? Get off my ride. You might scratch the exterior." He wiped down the Escalade as he spoke.

The girls were like vultures around Donnie. He didn't dare leave his ride unattended while they were around. He gave the girls a ride around the block just so he could get them to stop harassing him for a ride. They wasted time arguing over who was sitting up front.

When he got back to Jamal's place, Donnie blew the horn and stuck his head out the tinted window so Jamal and the crew could see it was him. When they realized the driver of the Escalade was Donnie, they came charging out. They were just as excited as Donnie was over his ride. Ron, Jamal, Lee, Travis, Sean, and Randy each gave Donnie a high five or a quick man hug. They all piled in. They were touching everything— adjusting the seats and the sound systems. Travis, Lee, and Jamal each took a turn sitting in the driver's seat pretending to drive. Donnie didn't complain. He was all smiles.

"Here, Ron," Donnie said, tossing his friend the keys. "Take it for a spin."

Everyone piled in, and the music volume went up. They stopped to chat with everyone they knew. They all stuck their heads out the windows, yelling to every girl they saw. When they reached the school grounds, they turned off the music and cruised through the campus slowly, speaking politely to the teachers and staff.

"Hello, Ms. Anderson. It's a beautiful day, isn't it?"

Ms. Anderson, walking inside with a briefcase and books, replied, "Make sure you're all in class on time. Oh yeah, and make sure you get a parking sticker. You don't want this nice ride towed." She walked toward the school building.

Ron tried to find a parking space.

"Damn! I forgot about that," Donnie said. "Let me out right here."

Ron had barely come to a complete stop when Donnie jumped out.

"What the hell?" Jamal asked.

"Yo, Ms. Anderson, wait up," Donnie called. He looked back at Jamal. "I'm going to get a parking sticker. I don't want my shit towed."

"Donnie, I don't have all day," Ms. Anderson said.

Donnie ran to catch up with Ms. Anderson, who was waiting near the door. "Where do I get a parking pass?"

Inside, Ms. Anderson was saying, *Thank God*. She's worried if the Escalade belong to any one else other than Donnie than it could mean something illegal involve. She was relieved when she saw who was inside, knowing the boys in the Escalade were good kids. They didn't hang with the wrong crowd or do drugs.

Donnie followed Ms. Anderson to the office for his parking pass.

"Does Ron have his license?" Ms. Anderson asked.

"Um, yeah," Donnie replied. He was trying to get away from Ms. Anderson before they got busted. Donnie, Jamal, and Lee were the only ones with driver's licenses.

Donnie believed his new ride would help him meet college chicks. He wanted to be just like Ron. At times, he wished he was Ron.

Donnie's vehicle would be full all the time with friends.

"Man, I bet this cost a fortune," Travis said to Donnie.

"I don't know," Donnie replied.

"Why you let Ron drive?" Travis asked. "Let me drive some."

"You don't have a license," Donnie replied.

"So! Ron doesn't either."

"Yeah, but if he gets pulled over, cops like him. They let him walk."

"Damn, why is, Ron that you can get away with murder in this town and they will let you walk?" Travis hit Ron playfully on his shoulder. "I bet you don't even know how lucky you are. You got everyone pulling for you to succeed in this small town. Don't let us down, man."

Ron was admiring Donnie's new ride and not paying any attention to Travis. "You lucky to have the parents you got," Ron said to Donnie. "Some of us are not so lucky."

Everyone got quiet.

Donnie broke the silence. "My grandparents gave me a twenty-five thousand-dollar credit card. Let's go shopping after school—my treat, guys."

They were all up for that. Jamal was concerned about how he was going to be able to hang out with Donnie and the crew without Hallie getting upset. He was already in hot water with her for not riding the bus with her. He declined the after-school shopping trip.

Donnie, Ron, Travis, and Randy knew Jamal wasn't coming because of Hallie. They all agreed he should break up with her now.

Hallie was outside waiting for Jamal. She started screaming before he could get out of the vehicle. "Where the hell you been? I'm getting sick and tired of your shit!"

Jamal made an exasperated expression at Ron and Donnie. He knew what they was thinking.

"Don't let that witch talk to you like that, man," Ron said.

"Go to hell, Ron," Hallie yelled, "and stay out of my fucking business!"

"When I do, I'm taking you with me," Ron shot back. He got out of the Escalade and slammed the door then walked away.

Travis and Randy looked at Hallie and shook their heads in disgust before walking away. Donnie put the parking sticker on his vehicle and went to class. Jamal's friends didn't hang around to watch Hallie verbally insult their friend.

"Quiet down," Jamal said in a calm voice. "You're making a scene. We can discuss this in private."

Hallie was still furious. "Don't tell me what to do, you son of a bitch. You can go to hell with your damn friends."

By this time they had an audience.

Jamal started walking away, shaking his head in disappointment and embarrassment. *My friends are right*, he thought to himself.

Hallie was screaming so Jamal could hear even though he was now a good distance away. "You better take your no-screwing ass on. With your tiny ass dick."

The principal showed up and put a stop to Hallie's tantrum, making the rest of the kids go to class.

Michelle watched. *I will never do that to Ron*, she said to herself. Michelle had tears in her eyes. She didn't like fighting or arguing.

Hallie spotted Michelle and yelled out to her. "Michelle, do you still want me to show you how to apply makeup?"

"Sure," Michelle said in a gentle tone, "if it's no bother."

"Come over to my place after school. I'll teach you to get your man, girl." Hallie laughed.

The school day came to an end. The guys waited for Donnie near his ride. Jamal didn't care anymore. No matter what he did, Hallie was going to bitch anyway, so he decided to go to the mall with his friends.

Donnie got his friends cell phones, jeans, tennis shoes, cologne, and CDs. After shopping and hanging in the arcade room, they went out to eat. They all were flirting with different girls. Playing the game who could get the most female phone numbers. It was unbelievable that Donnie was getting more phone numbers than Ron. For Donnie, this was the life. He had money, a new ride, great friends, and now he could pull more women than Ron.

The boys' favorite sound came on, and they all bobbed their heads to the beat. Everyone was picking up women except Jamal. He kept his cool. He didn't want word getting back to Hallie.

The evening was coming to an end. As Donnie pulled onto Baker Street, windows down and music blaring, kids ran behind them.

Jackie and Kathy were sitting on the porch. They saw the kids pull up. Donnie kissed Jackie on the cheek. Ron, Lee, Sean, and Jamal showed off the new cell phones and clothes Donnie had gotten them. Lee and Sean said their hellos.

"Randy and Travis have practice today. They're going to be late," Jamal said. "What'd you cook, Mom?"

"Spaghetti, corn bread, and slaw." Jackie said. "I made enough for everyone. Sean and Lee, y'all do your homework before you leave. I want to see it when you're done. You can take some food home if you like.

"Make sure you wash your hands before you touch my food," she yelled through the screen door.

The boys were already eating and going for more. Lee and Sean both agreed that Miss Jackie was the best cook in town.

Everyone was too stuffed to do homework. Jackie made them do it anyway. Sean and Lee took big containers of spaghetti with them for their munchies later on.

Donnie loved Ms. Jackie's cooking. His mother couldn't cook. She'd never heard of or eaten collards. Donnie only asked the chef to prepare cheeseburgers with all the fixings. For home-cooked meals, he just went to Ms. Jackie's. Donnie's mother had never wanted to learn how to do domestic housework. She was always reminding her family and friends she was a career woman, not a domestic housewife. That's why she paid for housekeepers and chefs.

"I wish my mom could cook," Donnie said.

"What for?" Jamal asked. "You have a chef."

"I want a normal life."

Ron agreed. "I would give anything to have a mother like yours."

"My parents never have time for me," Donnie said. "They're never at home. They didn't see me take my first step, hear me say my first words, or hear me cry at night for them."

"That's all you got to complain about," said Ron.

"Wow, man," Jamal chimed in. "That's nothing. Your parents love you. You get everything you want."

"Yeah, not everything," Donnie muttered.

"What is it you want?" Ron asked. "You have everything. Look at my life. Do you want to trade places?"

"Geraldine's been a real mother to me," Donnie said. "When I'm grown, I'm going to make sure she has everything she ever wanted. She will have a maid and a cook. She deserves it."

"You need to meet my mom, if you can call her that," Ron said. "A title should be earned and not given. Your parents and my mother are absent all the time. They have that in common. But your parents make sure you have food, a roof over your head, clothes on your back, and someone to watch over you. But most important, you have parents who show their love. My mother doesn't give a damn if we live or die. She goes MIA for months and never calls to check on us. So spare me the details of your so-called unloved life. I can't feel sorry for you. I'm too busy feeling sorry for myself. If you could live my life for one week, you wouldn't last. Some people just don't know how lucky they are. Thanks for the cell phone and stuff. I'm turning in."

The mood had changed. Donnie was upset at himself for stirring up bad emotions. "Yo, man, Ron, don't leave. I didn't mean to bring out … I mean, you know, I'm sorry. We still cool?"

"I wouldn't have it any other way. We still cool. I just need to be alone." With his head down, Ron kept walking.

Donnie held back tears. Jamal patted Donnie on the shoulder and said, "He'll be all right." Jamal knew that when Ron got emotional, he'd rather be alone.

Jackie could sense something was wrong when Ron walked by her and didn't say a word. "Are you all right, baby?" she asked in a concerned tone.

Donnie walked out next. Jamal stood on the porch watching his friends walk away until they disappeared.

"What happened?" Jackie asked.

"Everyone was talking about how great you are and they wished you were their mother. Donnie brought up how his parents equate money with love."

"Say no more," Jackie said. "Poor Ron."

"Vera has really messed him up," Kathy said.

Jamal knew she was right. "Yeah, Randy hates her guts. He's always saying he hopes they find her dead."

Jackie sucked in her breath. "Wow!"

"Sometimes when Vera's calling Ron names and hitting him with whatever she can get her hands on, Randy says he plots her death," Jamal continued. "He told me one night he went into her bedroom with a kitchen knife and stood over her. Ron caught him in time. He was close to killing her."

"My God!" Jackie gasped.

"I can't believe Ron would stop him," Kathy said. "She needs to die."

"Stop thinking like that," Jackie said. "A higher fate will handle her one day. I need to check on Ron to make sure he's all right."

"I wish Ron was our brother," Jamal said. "I look up to him. He has mad skills. Vera tells him he ain't ever gonna be anything in life, and he believes her. I hate that evil witch." Tears ran down his face, which was clenched tightly into an expression of anger and his fist was drawn at his side. He went back inside and closed his bedroom door.

He needed someone to talk to. He repeatedly called Hallie, who kept hanging up on him.

Jackie returned from checking on Ron. She sat on the porch with Kathy.

"Is he all right?" Kathy asked.

"He didn't want to be bothered," Jackie replied. She was relieved that he was okay.

Kathy switched the subject. "When was the last time you saw Gerald?"

"Last week," Jackie said. "He'll be here tomorrow night."

"You know he's not going to leave his wife," Kathy said.

"I don't want him to—as long as he pays my bills and takes care of my needs. I don't need you to keep reminding me that Gerald is not leaving his wife."

Kathy wanted to hear about Gerald and Jackie's lovemaking again. There wasn't anything new to tell, and Jackie was getting tired of discussing her and Gerald's sex life.

* * *

Michelle had new glasses with ultra light lenses, her braces had come off, and Hallie had showed her how to apply makeup. Now Michelle was listening eagerly to Hallie tell her about how to style her hair and update her old clothes to look more stylish.

Sometimes Michelle would cry herself to sleep. She believed she was the ugliest girl in the world. She would pray to God to make her pretty.

Hallie offered to let Michelle wear some of her clothes. She could switch at school so Kathy wouldn't see what she was wearing. Hallie taught her how to slow dance and gave her tips on what a man liked in the bedroom. She told her that men didn't like condoms; they liked it raw.

Once Michelle's makeup was applied, she put on one of Hallie's outfits—one that was tasteful enough for school. Her hair was combed into a ponytail sweep to the left side of her head. Baby hair flowed around her face. She looked beautiful. She didn't recognize herself.

Hallie was proud of herself. With a smile on her face, she walked up to Michelle and stroke her hair and face. "Mama's little baby all grown up," she said. Then she opened a button or two to show a little cleavage.

Michelle was excited. "Oh my God. Look at me. I can't believe it. This is me. I look pretty, more mature …"

Hallie interrupted her. "You look like an eighteen-year-old lady with class. Ron will take notice now."

"You think," Michelle said.

"I don't doubt," Hallie said. "I know, honey. He will come on to you.'"

"Hypothetically speaking," Michelle pressed, "suppose he doesn't."

"Ron doesn't turn down a pretty face," Hallie said. "Get real, girl. If he doesn't make a move on you, then go to plan C. With plan C, for sure you will seal the deal. He will be all yours."

"I want him so much," Michelle gushed. "I want him to be my husband. I want to bear his kids. I want to love him forever. And I want him to love me with all his heart."

"Okay," Hallie replied. "You're getting ahead of yourself. The kids, marriage, forever stuff—all this babble about love! We are talking about Ron."

"This not babble," Michelle insisted. "I'm for real. I love Ron with all my heart."

"Ron doesn't know what love is," Hallie said. "He has no heart to feel."

"Then I will give him mine," Michelle proclaimed. "And I will keep giving until he realizes he now has one. I want him, and no one's going to stand in my way. I mean no one. Look at me. I have the looks and the brains. I will have him."

"Oh my." Hallie looked at Michelle in disbelief. *Where did this girl come from?* She was thinking. *She might want Jamal next.* Hallie quoted to Michelle. "Socrates once said that the hottest love has the coldest end."

Michelle felt that tonight would be the night. Once her mom had fallen asleep, Michelle would sneak out of the house.

She arrived at Ron's door around 2:00 a.m.

Ron was surprise to open the door and see Michelle standing there. "If you're here to see my brother?" he asked. "He's in his room." *Damn, girl,* he thought, *Your mother will skin me alive if she knows you're over here. I don't know why she even thinks that way.* Ron pointed her to Randy's room. Then he went to his bedroom.

He didn't know that Michelle was following him. He went to his bedroom and swung the door closed without looking back. Michelle walked closer until he felt her presence. She placed her cheek against his bare shoulder moving it gentle and slowly across his back.

Ron was speechless and in shock. Finally, he broke his silence. "Are you crazy? Your mom and the whole damn neighborhood will be after me." He grabbed Michelle by the arm. "You got to go." He pulled her and walked quickly to the door.

"I'm not a little girl." She tried to kiss him on the lips.

He turned and pushed her away. "I can't," Ron said nervously. "I thought you were here for Randy. You got to get out of here now!" He pushed her out the door. Ron was standing inside.

"What's wrong with me?" Michelle asked from the other side of the door. "I'm not a little girl."

"You're not a lady either. I respect you, Michelle. You're like a little sister to me. Go home and don't try to grow up so fast."

When she was gone, he closed the front door and watched her through the window until she disappeared inside her apartment. Ron couldn't believe what had just happened. He pinched himself to make sure he wasn't dreaming. He couldn't tell anyone. Who would believe it anyway? Ron was lying in bed staring at the ceiling and just above a whisper, he said, "I hope no one saw her. That's all I need." He closed his eyes and asked God, "Please don't let me get in trouble over this girl."

Hallie saw everything. She knew firsthand what Michelle's plan was. After all, they'd discussed the plan earlier. She also knew that nothing had happened. Michelle wasn't there long enough. Hallie crawled back into bed. Hallie tried to get some sleep, but every time she closed her eyes, she pictured herself and Ron making love.

Ron had to come up with a plan to make sure Michelle got over her crush. He knew she was jailbait. Ron decided to hang out more with one of his female friends so it would appear like they were an item. Michelle would see them together and lose interest in him he hoped.

* * *

Vera was back in town, showing off her wedding ring and bragging on her husband. The kids were in school. Jackie and Kathy were outside when they saw Vera. She walked over with her hand flexed out, flaunting her tiny .25 carat ring. Jackie and Kathy both said it looked cheap.

To Vera, the ring meant getting out of the projects.

Vera was there to pick up her daughter and her belongings.

"Where's your husband?" Jackie asked. "Why didn't he come with you?"

"He's running our business," Vera replied. "He owns his own company, you know. He owns his own home in South Carolina. That's where we're going to live."

"That's where you been all this time?" Jackie asked. "You could have called and give a number where you could be reached just in case something happened to one of the kids."

"I know they're in good hands if you're watching them," Vera replied. "Oh hell, you do a better job than me." Vera laughed out loud. She was trying to act snobbish, as if she was too good to live in the projects now. "I'm just here to get my daughter."

"What about your boys?" Jackie asked.

"They're grown," Vera replied. "They can take care of themselves.

"They're not grown enough to live on their own," Jackie protested.

"I'm not taking grown ass kids with me. There's not enough room."

"I don't believe what I'm hearing," Kathy said.

"You know what, Vera," said Jackie. "I'm not gonna bite my tongue anymore. Her voice rose with anger. "If it wasn't for Ron, I would have called social services and the police on you a long time ago. That's right. Your son, Ron, begged me not to. You're going to regret this day. You get the hell away from me. As far as I'm concerned, you can leave little Lisa here."

"You're just jealous," Vera said.

Jackie was furious. She had tears in her eyes. "Of what! I can't believe this piece of trash."

Vera was twisting her hips as she walked away.

"Calm down, Jackie," Kathy cautioned. "Look at it this way. Ron will be rid of her for good. He can get a break from all those beatings and all the name-calling. I know I could use a break. Whenever Vera's in town, I can hear all the yelling, screaming, and cussing. It keeps me up at night. I feel so sorry for him I start crying."

"This is going to send him over the edge," Jackie said. "It's going to kill him. When it comes to Vera, that boy is very sensitive. I don't know why. I just don't know why." She was crying and shaking her head in sorrow.

They could tell Ron was home. Vera was yelling and cussing.

"Mom, why we can't go with you? I promise I won't be a problem." Ron asked.

"I'm not taking a dumbass with me."

"At least take Randy," Ron said.

"You don't tell me what to do, damn it. Get the hell out of my face, you stupid black ass fucker. Put my suitcase in that cab. You ain't good for nothing. Don't nobody want you. I wish you were never born. That's why I couldn't keep a man." Vera grabbed Lisa's hand to take her to the cab.

Lisa was trying to push away. "I want to stay with my brothers," she cried out. "Ron! Ron! I want my brother."

"Stop your whining," Vera snapped. "I got you a daddy. You gonna like it where we're going. Now shut up." Vera went back inside.

Michelle was listening through the walls to Vera yelling and hitting at Ron. She was crying and holding a pillow over her ears. "God make her stop," Michelle whispered. "Somebody make her stop please."

Hallie called Michelle. "Michelle, are you listening to this?"

"Yes," Michelle said. "Why does she always belittle him? He's so talented. I hate her."

"Hey, this is a good thing," Hallie said.

Michelle interrupted, "How do you figure?"

"Hear me out," Hallie said. "He's going to be depressed and hurt, so you can be there to console him. He won't be thinking clearly. You can have your way with him. Go all out. Do everything the sex video showed. You have to put it on him the first time. If not, he won't waste his time coming back. Tonight is your night. You better take advantage of it. Tell me everything tomorrow. Chow." She hung up the phone.

Jackie went to the cab where little Lisa was. "Baby, stop crying," Jackie said softly.

"I don't want to gooooo," Lisa cried.

"I know, baby," Jackie said. "I don't want you to go either."

"I want my brothers to go with me," Lisa sniffled. "I'm gonna miss Ron and Randy."

"Lisa, here's my number," Jackie said. "I want you to keep this. Never lose it. If anyone touches you inappropriately or mistreats you, call me. I will never change my phone number. Call me. I don't care what time it is or how far you are. I will be here for you." Jackie gave Lisa a big squeeze.

Little Lisa hugged Jackie and said, "I love you. I wish you were my mama." She sniffed, tears still pouring from her eyes.

Jackie held back her tears.

She then went inside Vera's house to stop her from hitting and yelling at Ron. Randy was still at school. Jackie grabbed Vera and pushed her out the door. "Why don't you hit on someone your own age," she yelled. "I've been waiting on this moment for a long time. Fight me! Cuss me! Call me names!" She pushed Vera. "You're going to regret this one day. You going to reap what you sow."

Vera hurried up and got in the cab.

Jackie went inside to console Ron. Tears ran down his face. "Why can't she just try to love me?" Ron asked. "I wish I was dead. No one loves me. No one cares."

Lisa, who had jumped out of the cab, burst into the house and ran past Jackie, straight to Ron. She hugged him and said, "I love you, I don't want to go without you.. I wish you could go with us."

"Lisa, get your ass in this cab," Vera yelled. "Let's go."

Vera tried to go back inside, but Jackie blocked her entrance. "Let the girl say good-bye to her brother."

"I'm glad to get out of this godforsaken place," she said as she got back into the cab. She yelled again. "Lisa, I'm not gonna call you again!"

Jackie went inside to get little Lisa. "I will always be with you," Ron was saying. "I love you, little sis."

Little Lisa's crying .I don't want to go. I want my brother. I want Ron, Eeeee she cried louder. Jackie swept her away to put her in the cab. "Remember what I told you, Lisa," she whispered.

"Let's go," Vera snap. "Don't be filling her head with any nonsense." Vera didn't look back as the cab pulled away.

Jackie went back inside to check on Ron. "I want you and Randy to move in with us," she said. "You know I have always considered you and Randy as my own."

"Thank you, Ms. Jackie. Right now I just want to be alone. I promise I won't do anything foolish. I'm too emotionally drained. I just want to rest."

"You can rest at home," Jackie said, "our home. Ron, you are special. Don't let anyone tell you different. And don't let Vera discourage you."

"The damage has already been done," Ron said. "If your own mother doesn't love you, then who cares?"

"I care. The neighborhood, your friends, little Lisa, and Randy—we all care. We are all here for you."

Jackie went home, and later, Jamal checked on Ron. They talked a little until Ron told Jamal he was all right; he wanted to be alone.

When word got back to Randy that Vera was in town and was having one of her moments with Ron, he was furious. He got a gun from Snake and started jogging home. "I'm gonna kill that bitch, and nobody going to stop me this time," he said in a rage."

When he got home, Vera had left fifteen minutes earlier. Without knowing this, he burst through the door with gun in hand. "Where are you, you evil bitch?" he yelled. "Come out here and pick on me. This is your lucky day. You going to die today."

Ron came out of his room. He was in a state of shock when he saw Randy holding a gun.

"I'm going to kill that bitch," Randy said, "and you're not going to stop me this time. So get out of my way."

"Hey, calm down," Ron said. "This is my problem, not yours. You don't need to be talking about killing our mother or anyone. Where did you get that gun?"

"Stop calling her mother."

"Put that thing away," Ron told his brother. "Don't let this take over your soul. Our mother is not worth you losing your soul."

"I'm sick of her coming back here after being gone for weeks, months, days and thinking she can treat you, us like a dog."

"I'm going to be all right," Ron said. "Where you get that gun? On second thought, I don't want to know; just get rid of it now."

"When I see her again, I will spit in her face," Randy said through gritted teeth.

"No, don't do that. She's still our mother. Besides, if it wasn't for her, we wouldn't be here."

"That's just like you" Randy said. "You see a bright light after every darkness. I don't know how you can defend this woman."

"You're carrying too much hate. This is not your war. If I'm not sweating over this, then why should you? This is our mother you're talking about killing."

"She's not my mother," Randy snarled. "And don't let me hear you use that word again. I don't know how you can call her that."

Ron looked at his brother and sighed. "I know I can't change your mind, and I'm not trying to. I just want you to promise me that you will never ever let your feelings about Vera make you go off and do something stupid. We can learn something from this."

"Like what?"

"Like never ever mistreat your family when you have one. Make good of our life and don't let Ms. Jackie down. She's our family now."

Randy perked up. "Yeah, boyeee. We are going to have a good time. I'm glad Vera's gone. I hope she never comes back. Jamal, Travis, you, and I playing pro football—rich and having all the honeys we want. We'll buy Ms. Jackie a big house and get her a maid."

Ron smiled at his brother's dreams.

"You and I will be so rich and successful. We will have enough money to get our sister back. Once we're billionaires that damn witch won't get a penny of our money."

Ron broke off Randy's rambling. "Yo, man, I'm tired. I'm going to my room to listen to some music and turn in for the night. Make sure you get that gun out of here before someone gets hurt."

"I will," Randy promised, "first thing in the morning. I'm going to stay here with you big bro. Have I ever told you I'm glad to be your younger brother. You're everything I want to be. I love you, man."

Ron smiled. "I'm glad you're my brother also. If I could be given a choice of families—the one I have now or a family with a great mom but different siblings—I wouldn't change it. You're the best brother I could have. If you ever need me, I'll be there for you. Now leave me alone so I can get some sleep and close my door behind you."

Ron's world was turned upside down the day Vera abandoned them. He lost all respect for women and any hope for himself. He gave up on life. He believed no one cared or could possibly love him. What Vera had instilled in his head had finally sunk in. Women just wanted him for sex. He wasn't good for anything else. He lay in bed crying, tossing, and turning. He had the radio turned up so Randy couldn't hear him sobbing. "Why doesn't anyone want me? Why can't someone love me? God, please just let me die. I don't want to live anymore. Just take me. No one loves me." He repeated these words over and over until he dozed off.

At three o'clock in the morning, Ron woke up restless, worried, and scared. He had a lot on his mind. One of those things was his sister. Would he ever see her again? What if Vera's new man was a sicko who preyed on little girls?

Ron wasn't a drinker, but he needed something to help him relax. In the refrigerator was Vera's wine. It didn't take him long to feel the effects. It was going to be a long, restless night. Randy was in a comatose sleep. Nothing could awaken him.

Ron heard a knock on the back door. He didn't bother to peek out the window to see who it was. Michelle was standing there with a coat on.Its the hottest night of the summer. He let her in. Nothing surprised him anymore. "What do you want, Michelle? I told you before I don't mess with kids."

"I'm not a kid," Michelle says. "Don't worry. I'm not here for that. I thought maybe you needed a friend after the day you had."

"Yeah. It's way passed your bedtime. Don't you think you better get back home before your mama finds out you're missing?"

"My mom took a sleeping pill. She's not waking up anytime soon."

"Well at least you have a concerned mother," Ron said, "unlike some of us."

Michelle spoke softly. "I wish I could take your pain. You know the percentage of dysfunctional families in the world today?"

"No, and I don't want to know either. I just want to know my sister's going to be all right. And will I ever see her again."

"You will see her again," Michelle said reassuringly. "You just have to put all of this behind you. You can start all over with a family of your own. You can get married, have some kids, and be a better person than Vera."

Ron switched the subject. He didn't know why Michelle was talking about kids and marriage. He was falling deeper into a depression. "You want to play some scrabble?" Ron was walking around only in his boxers. The alcohol gave him that I don't give a damn attitude."

Michelle followed him to the bedroom. She sat on his bed while he looked for the game. Michelle asked Ron. "Is it okay to take my coat off?"

"Oh, I'm sorry," Ron replied. "Let me take your coat."

Michelle stood up and turned her back toward him so he could assist with taking her coat off.

To his surprise, Michelle had on sexy red lingerie and smelled like strawberries. "Damn. You might need to keep your coat on." Michelle had picked up some weight in all the right places. Ron was doing everything to keep his composure. He couldn't concentrate for looking at her lips.

Michelle was tingling all over. She was in Ron's bedroom, and he was in his boxers and looking good. She was hoping he would make a move on her. She didn't realize Ron let women make the move on him first.

Ron knew Michelle had something on her mind other than talking and playing scrabble. He leaned back on his bed to see if she would put the move on him.

After a good time went by with nothing happening, Ron asked, "What do you really want here, Michelle?"

Michelle blushed. "I want you to want me."

"Why? What can you do for me? Are you a virgin?"

"No."

"I like my women experienced. You are a virgin, aren't you?"

Michelle lied. She leaned closer to get on top of Ron. She started kissing his face. She thought he had the most beautiful soft face.

Ron grabbed Michelle's long hair to push her face from his. He wanted to look her in the eyes so he could see her expression. "I hope you know what you're getting yourself into. I don't want a girlfriend or a baby. What we do in this bedroom stays here, okay?"

"Okay."

"You know you're making a big mistake," he whispered in her ear. He start licking around her earlobes and inside her ear canal and nibbling on her neck. He worked his way down to her breasts, where he sucked on them like a baby nursing a bottle. Michelle's body was soft, smooth, and a beautiful chocolate color. He moved one hand to caress the opposite breast. She closed her eyes and was taking deep breaths.

The more he kissed and sucked her breasts, the more she moaned. He took his tongue and made a circular motion around her navel, working his way down until his mouth was fully licking and sucking her clitoris. He put both hands on her bottom and pushed her hips closer to his face. Michelle couldn't contain herself. She had never felt this kind of pleasure before in her life. Her moans got louder and louder as she jerked and twisted her body.

Ron had never seen anyone show so much passion and excitement. He never performed oral sex on other women. They did him. He knew Michelle was a virgin, and he was going to keep it that way. He inserts his finger inside her while licking her all over. The other hand squeezed her small size breast. It was too much for her to take. She squealed with noises Ron had never heard before. It was making his penis harder and harder. She exploded with juices that he didn't know one woman could have so much of.

He rose up and kisses her on the lips and said, "You're a liar. I didn't think someone so innocent would lie."

"What did I lie about?" Michelle asked.

"I could tell you're a virgin. You couldn't handle a finger inside you. You know we can't do this again."

"What!" Michelle exclaimed. "Why?"

"I don't do virgins," Ron insisted. "I like experienced women. You're still a kid."

"What do you want me to do? I'll do anything for you. I'm not a kid."

"You've got to go," Ron said. "I have to be somewhere." Ron was going to see one of his female friends so she could get him off. He was trying to put Michelle out, but she was asking a lot of questions.

"Where are you going at this time of morning?"

"Listen to you," Ron said, "already acting like we're a couple."

"Are you going to see another woman?"

"I'm not going to lie. Yes. I got you off; now I got to get someone to get me off. Look." He held his long, hard penis in his hand. "It's so hard it hurts."

"Do you get all your girlfriends off the same way you got me off?"

"No, they're not virgins. I don't put my mouth where other men have been."

Michelle looked into Ron's eyes. "I will do whatever you want me to. Just teach me."

"Nope, I'm not going there with you. Don't come back here."

Ron assists her with her coat, and she put her arm around him and kissed him gently on the lips. "I promise next time I'll be better."

"Michelle, there's not going to be a next time." He pushed her away.

"Yes there will and you know it," Michelle replied. "You enjoyed me as much as I enjoyed you." She kissed him again and walked home. She had a smile on her face.

Ron couldn't believe how cocky she was. He was trying to figure out her attitude. *What have I gotten myself into?* He asked himself. *She's not that innocent girl we thought she was.*

Hallie couldn't wait to get the lowdown from Michelle. "Girl, tell me everything. Did you do it? Was he all that and then some? Tell me everything."

Michelle lied. "Nothing happened. We played cards, scrabble, and checkers. We talked."

"You're lying," Hallie said incredulously. "You were over there a long time."

"That's all he wanted to do," Michelle insisted. "He was too upset for anything else." She remembered Ron telling her that what went on in his bedroom stayed in there. She was going to be obedient to her man. She wasn't going to do anything to mess things up. *I'm not telling her anything,* she promised herself. *She'll try to use it against my Ron.*

Michelle continued sneaking over to Ron's apartment. He continued having oral sex with her. She knew he was seeing other women. She wanted it to stop. She wanted all of him. She went on the Internet and looked up every resource on how to please a man, how to get a man to fall in love with you, how to make love, and the best sex moves that drove a man crazy. She read books on how to make love like a pro.

Ron kept reminding Michelle that he didn't want a relationship. Ron never invited Michelle over; he never called her; and in public, he didn't knowledge her. He kept his distance. She would stay awake at night just to see when he came home and with whom. She would cry her eyes swollen whenever she saw him with another woman. She was desperate to have him be her first. She thought that, if she let Ron be her first, he would fall in love with her.

Tonight would be the night she would give herself to him. She soaked in her mother's strawberry oil. She slid on hot pink lingerie she'd ordered online. She stayed awake half the night waiting on Ron. He sometimes tried to avoid Michelle by not coming home at all. She would stay up all night long watching out for him. Her body craved him. It had been a long time since she was with him.

Before Ron could get through the door, Michelle sneaked up behind him.

"Shouldn't you be in bed? It passed your curfew."

"I've been waiting for you," Michelle replied.

"I don't feel like it tonight," Ron said. "So go home."

"We haven't been together in weeks," Michelle said. "You're never home."

"Go home." Ron was inside.

Michelle followed. She went to his bedroom, took off her coat, and flipped her long hair around.

Ron stood in the doorway to his bedroom and watched her perform.

"You're just like the rest of the girls," Ron said. "You're using me too. You're a tease."

"I'm wearing your favorite color. You like?"

"It looks good on you," Ron said.

Michelle walked up to Ron and started unbuttoning his shirt and kissing him. She put her tongue as far in his mouth as she could and twirled it around. She sucked his nipples as she unbuttoned and unzipped his pants. She then found her head between his legs, her mouth pulling, licking, and sucking on his hardness.

He didn't reject her. He let her take charge. He took his hands and held her head down and stroked her beautiful hair. Her mouth was warm and wet. He couldn't believe how good it felt. It felt different from the rest. He lay back and let her have her way. "Shhhhh … Oh, baby, don't stop. That's right. Keep going. Put it all in." His hardness grew harder in her mouth. He pumped in and out.

She could feel him swelling up more. His moans were making her hot and wet between her legs. Ron flipped her over and around so they could be in the sixty-nine position. This was a first for Michelle. She was always the receiver. Now she could give back and receive.

She couldn't hold back any longer. "Fuck me," she screamed. "Fuck me now! I want you." She pulled up and got on top of him. She grabbed his hard penis and tried to insert it inside her. "Please make love to me. I want to feel you inside me now. Fuck me, baby. I want you so much. Put it inside me now."

Ron flipped her over so he could be on top of her. With his face buried in her neck, he whispered, "This is all you want from me. You're just like the rest. You want it, you got it; you got it, baby." He first used his finger to penetrate her vagina until she was filled with her juices.

Michelle moaned with pleasure. "Fuck me now!"

Then he inserted his hardness inside her gently. It was easy to insert since she was so wet.

"Ouch!" Michelle cried out. "It hurts."

"You want me to stop?" Ron asked.

"No," Michelle cried. "It hurts so good. Oh, it feels so gooooood. I love you, Ron."

Ron wasn't listening. He was enjoying the best damn stuff he'd ever had. He'd never felt sex that was so hot and wet. She leaned her warm body closer to his so they could be as one. She placed both hands on his butt cheeks and push them toward her as she rolled to keep up with his motion. Michelle's moaning and groaning got louder. Ron was so turned on by some of the things she was saying in the heat of the moment. Michelle moaned loudly, and he yelled with pleasure with her. "Oh hot damn! This is some good stuff. It's good baby! This is the best …" He cut himself off before he could finish his sentence.

Michelle moaned and groaned with pleasure. She kept coming and coming.

"Oh, Michelle, baby, I'm … Oh shit, I'm coming." He knew he couldn't plump her wild and hard since this was her first time, so he was gentle with her. "Damn, you surprise me. You got some good stuff. I can't hold it any longer. I'm com … ing."

She felt him as he came. She went wild with pleasure. Michelle moaned. "I'm coming too!" She nibbled and sucked on his ears and neck. She inserted her finger in his anus. She licked his nipples and twirled her tongue inside his belly button, her breathing was getting heavier.

And then they exploded. He felt all her juices again. She felt his penis stiffen and getting harder again. For hours, they did it until they climax together and couldn't move. She was hurting, and his penis was tender. But they didn't have any regrets. It felt beyond good, beyond wonderful, beyond fantastic. She couldn't find the words to describe this feeling. She lay there with her arms wrapped around him tightly. She imagined what it would be like to be married to Ron.

Ron jumped up. "Michelle, you better go before you get caught. We got carried away. I should have asked you this before we got started. Are you on birth control?"

"Yes."

"Good. When you get home, soak in some hot water with Epsom salt. That should help with the soreness some. Make sure you don't tell anyone about us. How you feeling? Any regrets?" He pulled her up from the bed.

Michelle answered in a soft, sweet tone. "I'm okay. I feel good. I'm glad you were my first."

Ron kissed her and said, "Thank you for a great time. I've never had a virgin before. You could drive a man crazy."

After hearing that, Michelle felt special. She knew Ron cared for her. He acted concerned when he asked how she was doing. She couldn't stop thinking about their night together.

The more they got together, the better the sex got. Ron taught Michelle how to freak him, and she liked doing whatever it took to please him. She was in love.

Ron cared about her, but he didn't care enough to be faithful. He didn't know the meaning of love because he'd never felt it. He played around more. Michelle would see him at school with other girls. She was brokenhearted and cried a lot. She was depressed often. She stayed in her bedroom a lot with the door closed. She didn't have much of an appetite.

When they did get together, she made up for it. Michelle would be like a wild tiger in the jungle. They got together once or twice a month. By that time, her body was beyond craving. She was starving for his touch.

One night when they were together, Ron had other plans. The phone kept ringing. He wouldn't answer it. Michelle was suspicious. After their quick lovemaking, she knew he was trying to get rid of her. Instead of walking her to the door as usual, he told her to lock the door behind her. He then answered the ringing phone.

Michelle pretended she had left. She stood in the hallway out of sight but in hearing range.

"Yo, baby, what's up," Ron said. "Yeah, last night was great." After a pause, he continued. "I told you I would call. I just got in. I had some things I had to take care of." He was silent for a moment and then, "Damn, baby, I like that. You know you're the best. I'll be right over." He listened then replied, "Oh no, my Mom's home. She won't let me have women in my bedroom. And you know what happens when we together. You make too much noise."

Michelle made herself visible. Tears streamed down her face.

Ron was shocked. A frightened look crossed his face, and he slammed the phone down, cutting off the other party. Ron spoke nervously. "How long you been standing there? What did you hear? It's not what you think."

The phone started ringing again. Ron looked at the phone and then at Michelle. Michelle broke down and cried like a baby. She crawled into a fetus position. "I love you so much," she sobbed. "How can you do this to me? I gave you my soul. Why do you keep hurting me like this?"

Ron felt sorry for her. He had never seen anyone so emotionally upset over him.

She kept repeating, "I love you so much. I would die for you."

He'd never known what love felt like. He was all broken up to know he'd caused her pain. He reached for Michelle and held her in his arms. Holding back his tears, he said, "I will never hurt you again. I'm so sorry."

Michelle continued sobbing. Ron picked her up and laid her on his bed. He stroked her hair. "I'm so sorry. I didn't know anyone was capable of loving me. Mom always told me no one cared for me." Ron looked sad and hurt. He pulled her up to him, wiped her tears, and started kissing her like a delicate rose.

"You hurt me," Michelle said.

"I know. I'm sorry. You knew what you were getting yourself into. Tell me what to do to make this right."

"Don't hurt me again please," Michelle replied simply. "I love you so much."

"I know."

They made love all night long. The sun was coming up when Michelle sneaked through her bedroom window.

The next day, Kathy was talking to Jackie about Michelle. "She's been having an attitude lately. I tell you, Jackie, I don't know what's gotten into this girl."

"Did you bother to ask her?" Jackie asked. "It could be she met a boy and doesn't want you to know it."

"Nah, I don't think so. It has to be school. She's preparing for college at such a young age. I believe the pressure is getting to her."

"If you say so," Jackie said. "I think it's more than that."

"I can't talk to you," Kathy said in a huff. "You're always thinking Michelle's seeing a boy. My baby is still a virgin."

"You need to start thinking about birth control before she goes off to college," Jackie retorted.

Kathy changed the subject. "I haven't seen Gerald lately. What's going on with you two?"

Jackie leaned back in her chair. "He was getting too jealous and possessive. One night, he came over here banging and hollering, 'Open this damn door. I know you have someone in here.'"

"What!" Kathy exclaimed. "What did you do?"

"I opened the door before he woke up my kids. He pushed me aside and started searching my apartment. He swore he saw a black Escalade in front of my place."

"That's Donnie ride," Kathy pointed out.

"That's what I told him. He didn't believe me."

"He's married," Kathy protested. "What gives him the right to be possessive?"

Jackie sighed. "I know. I had a hard time convincing him it's over. He's been riding by checking on me."

"Whaaaaa! He's crazy jealous. Married men usually are. I would be careful if I were you."

Jackie shook her head. "I told you before, he's harmless."

Kathy raised her eyebrows but accepted her friend's assessment. "How did he react when you told him it was over?"

"He acted like nothing ever happened." Jackie took a sip of tea. "He wanted to make love. I had to put him out. He was trying to hang over here more often."

Kathy nodded. "He was hoping you'd change your mind. Y'all so childish. Do you miss him?"

"Yes I do. I miss him a lot."

"Do you love him?"

"I don't know how I feel. He told me he would leave his wife for me if it wasn't for his kids."

Kathy eyed her friend. "Jackie, don't tell me you felt for that."

"No, I didn't," Jackie assured her. "I wouldn't break up a family. His wife and kids are one half of him, and I'm the other half." Tears swelled up in her eyes. She whispered to herself, "I really do miss him. I hope he calls."

"Have you made any preparations for the graduation party?" Kathy asked.

"Yeah, I already ordered chicken, ribs, and hamburgers. I'm grilling corn on the cob. You can do the potato salad. Everyone's going to be here. You can observe Michelle and see for yourself if she likes one of the boys at the party."

"She is not involved with anyone," Kathy insisted. "Please stop saying that. I have to go check on her. She hasn't been out of her room since she got home from school."

"Tell Michelle hello," Jackie called.

Kathy went home to check on Michelle. Her bedroom door was lock. Knocking, Kathy called, "Michelle, are you hungry? Do you want to ride with me to Radio Burger Palace? We can get some burgers and talk. Michelle, do you hear me? Unlock the door. You haven't been locking it."

"I don't want to go," Michelle replied. "But you can get me a palace burger with fries and a large mango milkshake." She never opened the door for Kathy. Michelle was reading her Yale introduction welcoming package. For practice she took some on line college classes.

Kathy knew it was a good sign that Michelle's appetite was improving. She didn't have to worry anymore. Kathy went over to Jackie's to ask her to keep an eye on Michelle. She was going to the store for Michelle; it was that time of the month, she lied. Kathy didn't want Jackie knowing she was going to Radio Burger Palace.

"Well at least she's not pregnant," Jackie said. "I'm glad."

Kathy went to Radio Burger Palace just to see Gerald. She placed her order and hung around. She saw Gerald flirting with girls. Kathy got his attention. He recognized her as Jackie's friend and went over to her.

"You're always in some woman's face," Kathy said.

"Why do you care?" Gerald replied. "I'm in your face now." He was looking around when he said, "Where's your better half?"

"I'm not my better half's keeper," Kathy replied with a laugh.

"You're a smart ass." Gerald smiled. "I like that."

They were flirting with each other.

"I don't see you going over to my girl's house anymore," Kathy said. "What happened to you two?"

"What's it to you? Did she send you here to check up on me?"

"Nah, she don't even know I'm here."

Gerald eyed her. "Yeah, right. Look, we're starting to get busy. I have to go take care of my customers."

"I'm a customer," Kathy said, meeting his gaze. "Are you going to take care of me?" She handed him her phone number with a smirk on her face.

"You're Jackie's best friend, humm."

"She said you two have broken up. So anything goes."

"Yeah, you right. Anything goes."

"Are you going to call me?" Kathy pressed.

"I told you I take care of my customers." He walked away just to stop and chat with another woman.

Kathy got her order and left, saying to herself, *Whoa! He's fine as hell, hmm, and has the body to match it.* She hid the food in her oversize pocketbook so Jackie wouldn't know she'd been to Radio Burger Palace.

Michelle came out of her bedroom long enough to eat. "Mom," she said, slurping a gulp of her milkshake, "I don't want to go to Alaska this summer. I'd rather stay home with you."

"Your father is going to be very disappointed."

"I decided to take a summer class at Greensboro College. I'm sure Daddy wouldn't mind if I miss this summer with him in Alaska."

"I will let you call him and break the news," Kathy replied.

"I will," Michelle agreed.

"Well, do it soon. Don't wait until the last minute."

"Mom, I'm sure Dad won't mine. He'll want me to excel in my academics, right? Let me read my essay I've been working on."

After she's read it, Kathy beamed. "Baby, I'm impressed. I feel like an idiot. The whole time you were locked away in your room working on this? Jackie was brainwashing me into believing it was because of a boy. I admit I was suspicious."

"What if I were seeing a boy?" Michelle asked. "What would you do?"

"Hmm," Kathy sighed. "Let's not even go there. Your father and I want you to go beyond our expectations. Getting involved with someone right now would ruin all of our lives, especially yours. Just keep making us proud."

Michelle finished her food and went back to her room. She was halfway there to getting out of spending the summer with her dad. That would be too long a time away from Ron.

She was looking forward to the graduation party. It was the only time she could hang out with her friends. Jackie taught her how to do the latest dances. She was ready to party and show Ron she could get down on the dance floor. She was even thinking this could be their coming out.

Chapter twelve

The Last Party

This was the big party. It was Ron and Jamal's graduation party. It was going to be the party everyone would talk about. All their friends, some parents, and some of their teachers would be there.

Everyone came to say good-bye and take pictures with their town celebrity. Ron had gotten several football scholarships and even a call from the NFL. Everyone in Greensboro knew Ron would be famous someday. The NFL was making exception for Ron, He was just that good.

Jamal had to apply for a grant or student loan if he was going to college. He wasn't as lucky as Ron. He was disappointed, but he wouldn't let on. He didn't want his college debt to burden his mother. He wanted to handle his own finances when it came to his education. His mother would have enough to worry about when his brother went off to college.

Ron didn't let all this attention go to his head. He never gave college any thought. Nor did he return the call from the NFL.

At the party, everyone was asking each other what college they were going to and what major they were taking. The graduates were so excited to be getting out of high school.

Michelle got a scholarship for Yale. Everyone was joking with her and her mom about her young age and her brilliant mind.

Michelle kept her eyes on Ron. She grew uneasy every time a girl came near him. Ron wasn't noticing Michelle. It was still in his nature to flirt.

Jackie was barbecuing ribs and chicken. She served slaw, grilled corn on the cob, and potato salad, along with alcohol-free wine and beer, which made the teens feel grown up.

Everyone was dancing. When a slow song came on, Ron was dancing with another girl. Everyone's attention was drawn to the sound of loud arguing. It was Hallie cussing at Jamal. Ron saw Michelle staring at him with tears in her eyes. Ron stopped dancing and went over to Hallie. "Chill out," he said. "You're making a fool of yourself. This is a party. Why the hell are you even here?"

Jamal had already walked away. He went inside to his room. He was hoping Hallie would follow so the drama would be inside and not outside where the party was.

"Go to hell," Hallie said to Ron. "You don't tell me what to do."

"I'm tired of you always embarrassing my friend," Ron said. "If it's the last thing I do, one day I'm going to find a way for him to dump your drama queen ass. It's time for you to go. We're trying to have a good time." Ron grabbed Hallie by the arm to escort her by force from the party.

Hallie jerked away from Ron's clutches. "I'm not going no damn where, and this not your party."

Jackie butted in. "It's my party, and you're no longer welcome. Leave or I'll call the police."

"Ya'll all stupid," Hallie called. "I don't want to be here anyway." Leaning into Ron, she whispered in his ear, "Ron, I know your secret. You don't want to mess with me."

"Leave now!" Jackie yelled at Hallie.

"This party is boring anyway." Hallie left.

Ron saw Michelle rolling her eyes at every girl he talked to. She was showing her jealousy. Ron decided to leave before she acted on it.

Kathy was watching Michelle off and on as Jackie had advised, though she didn't want Jackie to know it.

Michelle followed Ron home when no one was watching.

"You know you shouldn't be here," Ron said. "You're going to be missed."

"Why did you leave the party?" Michelle asked.

"You know why I left."

"I want to hear it from you. Why did you leave?"

"I'm not up for drama," Ron said. "If that's why you're here, than you better leave."

"You told me you would never hurt me again," Michelle said. "I watched you flirting with girls. You acted like I wasn't there."

"Damn, Michelle, what do you want from me?" Ron felt exasperated. "You know we can't be seen in public. You knew what you were getting yourself into. I'm no good for women. I'm never gonna amount to anything." Ron's voice grew louder. "I gave you what you wanted. So now what the hell do you want?"

Michelle was crying. "I'm pregnant," she said softly.

Ron choked on his own saliva. He was trying to get his breath when he said, "How the hell did that happen? You told me you were on birth control." Ron was pacing around. "Who's the father?"

Michelle stood up and slapped him as hard as she could.

He grabbed her hand before she could strike again.

"How dare you ask me that? I gave you my virginity."

"I didn't ask for it," Ron replied. "You threw yourself on me. I told you I didn't want a relationship or a baby. Damn! Damn! Damn!" He hit his fist against the wall, knocking a hole in it. "Have you told anyone?"

"No," she said nervously.

Ron sighed. "I'll take you to get an abortion before anyone finds out."

"No!" Michelle cried. "I'm keeping our baby. It's a product of our love that we share together. You're going to be a father so get used to it. I love you more than life itself. We can get married."

Ron looked puzzled. "What soap opera have you been watching? I should never have messed around with you. You just fucking ruined me. Your father's going to kill me. Ms. Jackie's going to lose respect for me. I might lose my best friends."

Michelle walked up to him, kissing and trying to undress him.

He tried to pull away. "Stop! We can't do this ever again."

"Don't reject me now," Michelle replied. "The damage has been done. I want you now, and if you reject me, I will go and tell everyone at the party that I'm pregnant with your child." She was kissing him and undressing him.

Ron stood there emotionless. "You turned out to be a bitch," he said. "You planned this, didn't you?"

"Make love to me," Michelle said. "You know what I want done first." She undressed and lay on his bed, her legs spread wide. She placed both her hands on his head. She closed her eyes and pushed him into her. She repeated over and over, "I love you. I love you so much. I will do anything for you. I'm never going to let you go."

Ron couldn't resist much longer. The heat of passion made him give in to her erotica. He pulled himself up so he could get on top and inserted his hardness inside her. They went wild with pleasure.

"Damn, Michelle, you're good." He moaned and screamed her name over and over again. He hit the pillow beside her head and said, "I didn't expect this to happen. I do feel something for you. But it's not going to work." He was rubbing her belly and kissing it. "But you win, baby," he said. "You got me."

They hugged each other tightly and kissed.

"I've never had anyone to care for me the way you do," Ron said. "You have shown me over and over again, but I've refused to believe that anyone could love me. I can't wait till our baby is born. How many months along are you?"

"Four months," Michelle said. "This is what you need—your own family." She started kissing him all over so they could go another round. Michelle loved sex so much that sometimes Ron had to turn her down.

After they finished their third round, Ron jumped up before she tried for a fourth. "Michelle, baby, go take a quick shower before your mother realizes you're missing," Ron said.

They took a shower together.

At the party, Jackie and Kathy noticed that Michelle and Ron were missing. Kathy checked. Michelle was not at home. Kathy called Hallie, and no one answered the phone.

"She left with someone," Jackie said. "Just watch when she comes back—look around and see who else appears."

"I can't believe this girl," Kathy said. "Just when I was trusting her. Where can she be? Oh hell no. My God, I hope it's not who I think it is."

"Don't jump to any conclusions," Jackie cautioned." You should have had that sex talk with her last year."

"She will be going to her Daddy's if I find out she's sneaking around." She looked the crowd over.

Jackie said to Kathy. "I'm going to check on Jamal. I hope this little stunt Hallie pulled this time will finally make him see what she's really about."

Jackie walked into Jamal's bedroom. "Are you all right?"

"Yell, Mom," he said. "I know what you're going to say."

"So what are you going to do about her?" Jackie asked.

"It hurts me to even think about it. I try to shake her out of my system, Mom. It's so hard. I love her so much."

"This is not love," Jackie said gently. "Love can be a beautiful thing if you have the right partner. It's giving and receiving. This relationship with Hallie—you're the only one who's giving. No one should be treated the way she treats you."

"I love her so much," he protested.

"No you don't. You're in lust. You young people confuse the two. You don't know what love is because you've never experienced it. I can tell you this—it's not what you and Hallie have. This girl doesn't love you. She sees you as her way out of the projects. You already know she will cheat on you. Why would you want a woman you can't trust? She's no good, son. You have to end this now."

"I know, Mom." Jamal looked sad and disappointed. He knew Hallie was using him. "Mom, I've been thinking for a while now. Since I didn't get a college scholarship, I want to join the military. I need to get away. Maybe this will give me time to think and put some distance between Hallie and me."

"I agree. Getting away and not seeing her will help you get over her quickly. It's an old saying—out of sight, out of mind. I think joining the military is a good idea." Jackie smiled at her son. "Are you coming back to your party?"

"Nah, I'm going to call it a night," Jamal said. I can't face my friends right now. I have some more thinking to do."

"Well, it seems like my guests of honor have left their own party.

"What do you mean?" Jamal asked.

"Donnie, Lee, and Sean left with some girls they picked up at the party. Ron disappeared after he put Hallie out, and we can't find Michelle."

"She's probably at home."

"No, we checked. I believe Michelle has a boyfriend. Kathy doesn't believe it. But Michelle's not a virgin anymore."

"How do you know that?" Jamal asked.

"The way she's been acting lately."

"Man! That's hard to believe. I feel sorry for whoever he is."

"I bet you Hallie had something to do with it," Jackie said. "Michelle and she have been hanging around each other quite a bit. No telling what she's been brainwashing that child with."

"Mom, please don't blame Hallie for everything that goes bad around here."

"Oh God, I can't believe you're taking up for her again." Jackie shook her head in disbelief. "I better leave. I hope you feel better." Jackie walked out and slammed the door.

Jamal made sure his mother was out of hearing range before he picked up the phone and dialed. "Don't hang up. I got some good news. I talked to my mom, and she thought it would be a great idea for me to join the military. Once I pass basic training and get stationed, then we can get married. We better not tell anyone our plans just yet. They might try to talk us out of it again." He listened for a minute and then said "The last day of school." He paused. "Uh huh, yeah." After a moment, he whispered, "I love you too. baby."

Chapter Thirteen

A Family Falling Apart

Michelle showed back up at the party and didn't care who noticed that she had been gone.

"Where have you been, young lady?" Kathy demanded.

"Home," Michelle lied, annoyed that her mother was asking her such childish questions. She walked away.

Kathy followed Michelle. "You were not home. I checked. You were not anywhere to be found, young lady," she said with anger.

Michelle went home, still not giving an answer.

"I demand an answer from you now," Kathy said, following her. "Are you messing with boys?"

"Stop treating me like a child," Michelle said, her voice rising in frustration. "I'm fifteen years old. I'm sick of you always over my shoulder. I can't even hang out with my friends. I don't have to tell you every step I make."

"How dare you raise your voice to me?" Kathy replied, her eyes narrowing. "You are still a child. I'm responsible for you. As long as you're' under my ..."

Michelle interrupted her before she could finish the sentence. "What mother? You going to put me out? Is that what you're about to say! Good because I'm leaving anyway. Ron and I are getting married. So I won't need to live here anymore."

Kathy was in shock. "What the hell did you say?! Have you been messing with Ron?" She took Michelle by the shoulders and shook her. "Answer me. Are you messing with him?"

"Stop it. Stop shaking me. I'm pregnant," Michelle screamed at her mother and jerked away.

Kathy slapped Michelle. "Get out," she said. "I can't look at you anymore. All this investing in your education going down the drain."

"That's just like parents," Michelle replied. "You try to live your dreams through us. You tell us when to crawl, eat, and sleep. Oh, now you can tell us when to grow up and what boyfriend I can have."

"He is a loser, Michelle," Kathy said, crying now. "He lives here in the projects. He has nothing to offer you, and he's too old for you."

"He is not a loser!" Michelle screamed. "And never ever call him that again. He got an offer from the NFL. He loves me, and I love him unconditionally. No one understands him like I do."

"He has problems—emotional baggage. He can't love. He doesn't know how."

Michelle looked at her mother. "I taught him how to love. He needs me, and I'm going to be there for him. No one's going to take our love away. You are not going to dictate my life anymore."

"Your father is going to kill your little so-called boyfriend," Kathy shot back. "So enjoy him while you can. This is a damn joke. You're a child. You taught him about love."

"I'm not a child!"

Kathy went to her bedroom and slammed the door. She called Jackie to break the terrific news to her. Then she called Tony.

"What!" he yelled. "I knew something like this would happen in your care. You should have let me have custody in the first place. This is your fault that this is happening. Has she had the abortion?"

"No," Kathy replied.

"What the hell are you waiting for?" Tony exclaimed. "She is not having this baby. She knows that, doesn't she? She's just a baby herself."

"She's going to be furious," Kathy told him. "She wants to keep it."

"I don't give a damn what she wants," Tony said. "She's only a child. We are the parents. We think for her. I'm wiring you some money. Take care of it before I get there. She's coming back with me—before you let something like this happen again. How dare you let this happen? You haven't been watching her properly. You let this happen to my daughter. Damn you! Damn!" He threw the phone against the wall.

In the back ground, Kathy heard Tony's wife ask "What's wrong honey?"

"That damn stupid ass woman let Michelle act wild. Now she's pregnant," Kathy heard him say before she hung up the phone.

Kathy broke down and cried.

Michelle went to Ron's house and broke the news to him that her parents knew.

Kathy was utterly devastated and in shock. She didn't care that Michelle spent the day and night with Ron.

Michelle was on a cloud. She had it all. She'd gotten Ron, his baby, and freedom from her mother. She was free to live her life with Ron.

Ron was happier than he'd ever been. He took a job at the library and called the NFL board for an interview. He stopped cheating and gave Michelle whatever she wanted and needed.

By this time, everyone knew about their relationship, and no one cared except her parents. Girls thought Michelle was one lucky girl. She had tamed the beast. It wasn't unusual to see a young girl pregnant in the Hamptons.

Kathy knew this abortion was going to devastate Michelle. She tried to prolong it as long as possible, hoping Tony would change his mind. Kathy had told Tony to let Michelle have her baby. Michelle could still finish school, and Kathy could help Michelle raise the baby. Years ago, Tony would have never considered abortion an option. Kathy had a lot on her mind, such as trying to figure out why Tony was telling her not to let Michelle know that he was the one enforcing and paying for the abortion.

I *could raise this baby until they get on their feet*, she thought. *Ron is going to be famous one day.* He had already done local commercials. He was very attractive. He could be a model or an actor or both. *Maybe if I call Tony back and tell him Ron got an interview with the NFL executives*, she reasoned, *he may just change his mind. This could be Michelle's and my way out of the projects.*

Tony and his wife lived in a nice home, drove a nice car. Their kids attended private school. *Look how I'm living*, Kathy thought. *All he wants to do is take Michelle. Then I'm stuck here in the projects with no other way out.* She decided that this could be her only chance. She could be the mother-in-law of a famous NFL player. She could see them all living in a mansion, driving fancy cars, traveling all over the world, and meeting other famous celebrities. *I might even get to date or marry someone famous*, she fantasized. *This could be my chance only chance to get out.* Waiting on Michelle to graduate from college as a doctor would take years—years Kathy may not even have. Kathy woke up from her daydreams.

Tony called weeks later to check on Michelle. "How's Michelle?" he asked.

"She's okay," Kathy said nervously. "I didn't go through with the procedure."

"What!" Tony exclaimed. "What the hell are you waiting for?

"I was thinking," Kathy began. "Ron is very talented. He got an offer from the NFL. Look, our daughter could get married to a famous athlete who could put us on the map. He could be rich and famous."

"What the hell are you doing, Kathy? For once, stop thinking about yourself. She needs her own identity. Do you know how many divorces there are today with young pro sports couples. At least she will have her own career. I'm not going to let you ruin her life. Now you take care of this situation now! Her education is more important than your greedy plans. For once, stop thinking about yourself and put our daughter first. You got the money, so take care of it.

"Remember," Tony added, "Do not tell her I'm insisting on this abortion. I'll be there for her graduation. Have her things packed. She won't need many clothes. We're taking her to buy a whole new wardrobe. We fixed up her bedroom so it could be more mature. When she enters college, we're going to move close by the first year, so she won't get homesick. You don't need to call the first few weeks after I pick her up. It will only remind her of this dreadful ordeal."

He cleared his throat and continued, his tone turning threatening. "If you don't take care of this little problem, I will cut you off from the extra money I've been sending you. Do you understand me? I will let you know when you can talk to her again. I don't want her getting any ideas about going home."

"You son of bitch," Kathy cried. "I know what you're do ..."

She heard a click signaling that he'd hung up on her.

Kathy hated Tony right now. He was trying to turn Michelle against her. *She will think he's a better parent than me. She will blame me for her abortion. He's treating me like this is my fault.*

This could happen to anyone, she consoled herself. *It doesn't mean I'm a bad or unfit parent. I did everything right. I did.* Kathy broke down and sobbed.

She hated doing this to her. It was going to break her heart. She didn't want to force Michelle to get an abortion, but she had no choice. She needed that extra money to support herself.

The following morning, Kathy made an appointment for the procedure to be done. Ron was at work. Kathy made Michelle move back home. She threatened her with the reminder that she was still a juvenile and Ron could be prosecuted for statutory rape. Michelle did not want Ron to get in any trouble.

Kathy told Michelle she had made an appointment for her to have an abortion. Michelle sobbed. "no!" she screamed. "No! You are not going to take my baby."

"You are too young to be raising a child," Kathy said. "You're only fifteen."

"I'm not a child," Michelle insisted. Ron and I are going to be married."

"He can't marry you. You're not old enough."

"I'm not going to let you kill my baby!" Michelle begged, "Please don't do this. I can feel my baby move." She took Kathy's hand and placed it on her stomach. "Feel your grandchild move. This is your grandchild you want to murder."

Kathy jerked her hand away and backed up so she wouldn't bond with her unborn grandchild. She turned her back so Michelle couldn't see her emotions. "This has got to be done," she said quietly.

"Please, mom," Michelle begged. "Please don't do this. Let me keep my baby, please. Please! Let me have my baby. I will do anything. If you want me to stop seeing Ron, I will." She fell on her knees and grabbed her mother's lower legs. "Please don't kill my baby," she sobbed. "Please don't kill my baby."

Kathy moved from Michelle's grip and disappeared to her bedroom. This was tearing Kathy up inside.

Michelle lay on the floor in a fetal position after her mother broke away from her. She cried until there were no more tears left. "Please, God, don't let her kill my baby," she said. "Let me die if she takes my baby. Please let me die if she kills my baby. Please, God." She repeated this refrain until her voice became hoarse.

Michelle didn't speak to her mother the next day. Tears streamed down her face as they drove to the abortion clinic. They both were quiet. Kathy felt that, once this was all over, things would get back to normal. She would have her little girl back.

Kathy made it clear to Michelle to agree with the abortion by telling her no NFL will sign Ron if they knew he got a fifteen year old pregnant.

When Michelle was wheeled from the recovery room, Kathy tried to comfort her. Michelle pushed her mother away, looked Kathy in the eyes, and said, "I will always hate you for this. Don't you touch me. Don't you ever touch me. I hope you die for killing my baby. You will never take my love for Ron from me. I will always love him, and we will be together someday."

"That may be so, but you won't be seeing him anymore. You're going away to stay with your father. If you don't want Ron's life ruined, you'd better cooperate. No NFL or any pro sports wants a rapist on their team. You may hate me now, but you will thank me later. This is for your future."

In the car, Kathy headed home. "When we get home, pack the things you need," Kathy told Michelle. "I don't want you calling or trying to make any kind of contact with Ron. I love you. That's not going to change.

You knew you were too young, and we were not going to approve of this relationship. You will not …"

"Shut up!" Michelle cut in. "Just shut the fuck up!" I heard you the first time. I hate you!" Michelle was angry. She was thinking about taking the steering wheel from her mother and forcing their car head on into oncoming traffic.

She focused on Ron. She stared out the car window. So many thoughts were running through her head. Should she jump from the moving vehicle or kill Kathy while she slept? Should she run away with Ron and never come back?

She remembered what Kathy had said. Contacting Ron could cause him to go to jail for rape. Now she would have to stay away from the man she loved. *I'll graduate college early and come back for Ron*, she told herself. *We will be together no matter what. I will be of legal age. And no one will be able to keep us apart again—no one!*

When they arrived at home, Michelle went to her bedroom and slammed the door as hard as she could. She looked out her bedroom window into Ron's and cried. She imagined what her baby would have looked like.

For days, Michelle avoided Ron. She was depressed and quiet. Ron tried to contact Michelle, but Kathy refused to let him talk to or see her.

His last message was, "Tell her the good news. I'm flying to New York to meet with the Jets coaches. I want you and Michelle to come with me when I sign the contracts. While I'm there, I have an offer to do a male runway and potato chips commercial. Man, I have big dreams for us—for Michelle and me—and of course you too, Ms. Kathy. We are going to have it all. The sky's the limit." Ron was excited. For the first time in his life, Ron knew what it felt like to be happy and in love.

Kathy didn't relay any messages from Ron to Michelle. Nor did she tell Ron about the abortion.

Michelle's father flew in and left with Michelle without her going to her own graduations ceremony. She didn't get to say goodbye to her friends.

"Flight US Air to Alaska is boarding at gate 122," the loud speaker announced.

Michelle grabbed her overnight bag and walked away from Kathy without saying good-bye.

Kathy walked up to Michelle. "Will you ever forgive me?" she asked.

Michelle kept walking without saying or looking at Kathy.

"No matter how you feel about me," Kathy said, her voice breaking with emotion, "I will always, always love you."

"Don't worry," Tony said. "She'll come around. She'll call you once she realizes this was the right thing to do. I'll keep you up with her progress." Tony hugged Kathy then got on the plane.

Kathy got back on the freeway heading home. She pulled up to her apartment.

Before she got out of the car, Jackie was there to console her. Kathy broke down. "My daughter hates me," she cried. What have I done? She's never going to forgive me."

"Don't say that," Jackie replied. "She will come around one day. She will; I know it." They both sobbed.

Ron heard from Hallie that Michelle was gone and had had an abortion. He was deeply hurt. Ron couldn't believe Michelle would do this to him. He isolated himself and went into a deep depression. He didn't eat, sleep, or bathe for weeks.

Michelle wasn't doing any better. Tony had to get her some psychological help.

Ron just stayed lock up in his room. Jackie kept checking on him and trying to console him. "Ron, you can't give up on life," she said. "Michelle would want you to move on."

"Like she did," Ron retorted bitterly. "It was so easy for her. She hasn't called. She wasn't mature enough to tell me about the abortion. She didn't even say good-bye."

"What about the contracts you were going to sign with the Jets?" Jackie asked.

"I'm not going to waste my time or anyone else's," Ron said. "My mama was right. I'm good for nothing. No one could love me—no one."

"Stop talking like that," Jackie replied. "Michelle loves you. You knew she was too young. She was underage. She had no control over her life. Her parents made the decision for her."

"That's not good enough," Ron answered. "She went against them on other issues. She could have fought harder to keep our baby. I would have done anything for her. For once I thought I had found it."

"What? Found what?"

"What my mom hid from me. All my life I've searched for the meaning of love—what it felt like and how I would know it."

"It wasn't hidden," Jackie said gently. "It's been here all along. Michelle showed you the meaning of love, and you got to feel it, sense it, and embrace it. So next time you will know it."

"There won't be a next time. The only reason my life had purpose was my baby." Ron was choking back tears. "I guess I'm not good enough to have a baby."

Tears swelled up in Jackie's eyes.

"Ms. Jackie," Ron said, "take care of my brother for me."

Chapter Fourteen

Saying Goodbye

"Ron, I'm here for you too. Let me do my job and take care of both of you. Don't go off and do anything …" She stopped herself midsentence and wrapped her arms around him, patting his back as he wept.

"She never loved me. She killed my baby," he sobbed. "She killed my baby. She up and left me without a good-bye. She used me."

"She'll be back one day and you will know the truth," Jackie soothed. "Things aren't always what they seem. She cared a great deal for you. And we love you."

"I know you do, and thank you for everything. I got to get out of here. Everything here—this apartment, this neighborhood—reminds me of her."

"Where will you go?"

"I don't know. Don't worry about me. I can take care of myself. Just look out for my brother."

Ron left, and leaving became his pattern. No one would hear from him for days, weeks, or months. He didn't realize that he was doing exactly what his mother had done—disappearing without notice. Ron didn't care anymore about himself. He wanted to stop living. He started drinking and doing drugs, He never signed his million-dollar contract. Ron moved from one woman's house to another's. His taste for women went from classy to trashy. He stayed high or drunk. He wouldn't work. He would drive one woman's car to meet another. This was a continuous cycle.

No one knew how to locate Ron. He was always moving. He knew how to locate his friends if he wanted to .One particular time; he met Jackie and some of his friends to see Jamal off at the airport. Jamal was leaving for basic training in California. Ron looked like a vagrant. His friends were happy to see him but sad to see him in the shape he was in. They reached out to help him. He pretended he didn't need it. They hadn't seen each other since graduation. Everyone had been going his or her own separate way.

Ron had a nervous energy. He couldn't stay in one place too long. So he was the first to leave. Jamal was teary eyed as he watched his best friend walk away. Randy begged his big brother to come home with them. Ron refuses.

All of Ron's friends and associates wanted him to get his act together except for one person Hallie. She was gloating about Ron demise. Hallie wanted no part of the little get-together to see Jamal off. She said her good-byes earlier.

More visits to the airport were on the horizon. Donnie was the next to leave. His parents made him go off to a prestigious university overseas. They didn't give him a choice. They felt he'd had enough time to outgrow his identity crises and take his future more seriously. It was time for the future president of the United States to start learning to be who he really was.

Donnie didn't put up a fuss. He was outgrowing his friends in the projects. Donnie received five million dollars from his Granddad as a going away gift. He had his parents buy Geraldine a loft home in a gated community. He would send her a check every week for living expenses. Donnie never tried to contact any of the people he once called friends. He met new ones in college.

The neighborhood was changing. Baker Street was not the same. The neighborhood kids grew up and left. Now the neighborhood was back to its original status—gangs, drugs, and break-ins were taking over the neighborhood again. This new generation of kids was different. They talked back and had no respect for Jackie or any adult.

Jackie's only concern was Travis and Randy. She still hadn't given up on Ron. Jackie and Kathy were sitting on the porch when a suspicious car rode by. Jackie didn't chase it. They got up and ran for safety.

Kathy was still feeling sad and lonely. Tony wouldn't return her calls to let her know how Michelle was doing. Kathy was still hurt by the decision Tony had pressured her to make. She couldn't forgive herself.

Kathy wanted to go clubbing to have some fun and meet someone. Tony wasn't having sex with her anymore. He had no reason to visit now that Michelle lived with him. Jackie didn't like clubs. She was still trying to get over her heartache over Gerald.

Not wanting to go clubbing by herself, Kathy went to Radio Burger Palace alone. She flirted with Gerald and invited him over, promising it would be worth his time.

Gerald never turned down a pretty face. Late that night, Gerard arrived on Baker Street. Instead of going to Kathy's, he found himself at Jackie's door. Jackie missed him so much that it didn't take long before they were ripping each other's clothes off. They both missed each other, and it showed.

Gerald was feeling good about himself again. He had gotten back the one who had gotten away. He had never had a woman dump him before. He was the one who did the dumping. Jackie's leaving him had been a blow to his ego. Now he was on top of his game again. He had once told Jackie that they would always be together.

This time things between Jackie and Gerald were different. Jackie had hurt him. He now put her in the same category of his other women. He had a day he spent with each woman. Jackie's day was Sunday, which meant he would spend one or two hours with her. His excuse for not staying longer—Monday was a rough day at work. He told Jackie not to discuss him with her friends. The weekend woman was Gerald's main lover. He could stay overnight. His excuse to his wife was that Radio Burger had been busy; he had to work all night to do paperwork. Jackie wasn't the weekend lover anymore.

She knew she had made a mistake taking him back. He was acting like a real jerk to her. The phone rang at Kathy's. It was Gerald on his cell phone. "I'm walking up to your back door," he said. "Have it open so no one will see me."

Kathy and Gerald had been involved with each other for months. Kathy had fallen in love with him. She was jealous of his involvement with other women. She would start arguments with him when she saw him sneaking out Jackie's back door. When Gerald was breaking in a new woman, he wouldn't come around her for months. Kathy would drive by his house, leave notes on his car, and call his house and workplace and hang up continuously. She followed him going to meet women. She sometimes confronted them.

When Gerald found out she was confronting his women, he left her alone. He was still seeing Jackie, which drove Kathy crazy. She cried all the time. She was depressed. Jackie assumed her mood swing was over Michelle. Kathy was buying Gerald jewelry and clothes. She would beg him to come over and promise she would never confront his girlfriends again.

Of all the women Gerald had, he considered Kathy to give the best blow jobs. She was the only one who let him do whatever he wanted to do to her. He was constantly reminding Kathy she don't own him and that he was not leaving his wife and that she better not go near his house or family. Kathy was good in the bedroom, so he put her on the weekend list.

Jackie still didn't know about Kathy and Gerald, and Kathy was becoming more and more jealous of Jackie. She spent less time with Jackie, only going around Jackie to solicit information about her and Gerald.

On a couple of occasions, Gerald had snuck out Jackie's back door and into Kathy's front door in the same night.

Chapter Fifteen

Drama of all dramas

Basic training was over. Jamal called his mother and told her he had volunteered to go on a special assignment for the military. Jackie understood.

When Jamal called Hallie to tell her about volunteering she wasn't so understanding. She gave him an ultimatum—either he would come home now so they could get married or else. Jamal tried to explain that this was for their future. She yelled and called him names as usual.

"It's over," she said. "I never want to see you again."

"Hallie, listen, it's just for nine months," he reasoned. "After this assignment is over, we can get married. I promise. Nothing will stand in our way."

"Nine months," Hallie yelled. "That's too long! Are you crazy? You had no business volunteering without my permission."

"Calm down," Jamal said. "If we're going to do this, we need money. So taking on a few extra assignments will do us both some good. You need to know that I'm doing this for you. If we're going to get married, you need to grow up."

"Who the hell are you telling to grow up?" Hallie snapped. "If you're not here in the next two weeks, I'm giving it up to someone else."

"You know what, Hallie," Jamal said. "I'm tired of all your bullshit. Go ahead. Do what you do best. I'll see you when I see you." He hung up on her.

Hallie was shocked. Hallie called one of her girlfriends. "Guess who I just finished talking to? He's been listening to his mother again. Instead of coming home after his basic training, he's telling me he can't come home now for nine months. I know Jackie's telling him something." She paused. "Yeah, she's still trying to break us up. Once we're married, I'm going to make sure we move far away so she won't see or hear from him again. She thinks she's going to move in with us. That's so not going to happen. Hmm, I'll show her." She listened for a moment. "Hell no! I'm not having any babies. It messes up your shape as you get older. Hey, girl, I got to go. My mom's home. Chow."

Jamal didn't call Hallie or his mother for months.

Jackie was hearing rumors about Ron, and none of them were good. She found him staying in a boarding house that reeked of a foul smell. Winos, drugs addicts, and the homeless stayed there. When Jackie saw Ron, she barely recognized him. He had lost a lot of weight, he was dirty-looking, and he smelled. Ron was sating on the porch when Jackie arrive.

"When was the last time you ate?" Jackie asked.

Ron didn't look at her. "I'm not hungry."

"Yes you are, and you need a bath. Let's go."

"Where are we going?" Ron asked, making no move to get up.

Jackie placed her hands on her hips and stood her ground. "You are coming home with me, and you are not going to say no this time. Look at you. You know you don't have to live like this."Jackie was mad and her voice rose as she continued. "You gave up everything. You had it all. Why! Tell me why you bringing yourself down like this, doesn't make sense."

Her tone softened and she offered Ron a hand up. "Once you get a bath, and I fatten you back up, you're going to college. I'm not going to let you finish destroying yourself—not while I'm alive."

Ron was quiet while Jackie drove them home. Jackie bought Ron some new clothes and cleaned him up.

Overjoyed to see his brother, Randy caught Ron up on all of his sports activities he was into at school.

Ron still wasn't the same. He was sick a lot. Jackie told him she was taking him to the clinic for a physical. She was concerned about his health.

Hallie was still upset. She was getting angrier as time went by. Jamal hadn't called her. She tried to reach him but to no avail. Hallie repeatedly called Jackie to ask, "Has Jamal called? Have him call me."

Nothing gave Jackie more pleasure than to say, "Yes. I heard from him, and he's doing well. He's meeting new people."

Jackie's tone was smirky as she told Hallie this. After Jackie hung up, Hallie called her a stupid bitch. By now it was no secret to anyone who knew Hallie and Jackie how they felt about each other. They were like a time bomb about to explode.

* * *

Kathy was feeling insecure about her and Gerald. He hadn't been around her for weeks. She was curious to know if Jackie had heard from him. "Have you seen your boy lately?" she asked.

"Yeah," Jackie told her. "We went out to dinner."

Upset—Gerald had never taken her out—Kathy replied, "Really, mmm-hmm. Who paid for it?"

"He did, and we went to a drive-in movie afterward."

"You know he's not going to leave his wife—not even for you," Kathy reminded her. "I don't know how you can live with yourself messing with a married man who has kids."

"I don't want him to leave his wife," Jackie replied. "I know Gerald is no good."

"Why are you wasting your time with him?" Kathy persisted. "I wouldn't."

"For the sex, sweetheart—only for the sex."

"Mmm," was all Kathy could reply. She was so mad she interrupted her visit and went home.

Kathy started calling Gerald at his home and workplace and on his cell phone. He wouldn't return her calls. Kathy would lie in bed unable to sleep. She would constantly jump out of her bed to peek out the window trying to catch Gerald. Sometimes at four o'clock in the morning, she would drive around looking for his car. She knew where all his old flings lived and where he hid his car, but she couldn't find the new girlfriends. She would ride for hours all over the city looking for Gerald.

One night as Gerald was sneaking in Kathy's back door, Hallie saw him. Hallie made sure she stayed awake to see what time he left. This was too good to be true. She couldn't wait to see Jackie's expression when she found out she and her best friend were sharing the same man.

After that, whenever Hallie saw Jackie and Kathy sitting on the porch together, she would laugh out loud. Neither one of them knew why she would do that; nor did they care.

Hallie was still fuming that she hadn't heard from Jamal. She started hanging out just to find a sex partner until Jamal came home. She saw Ron hanging out, and he was looking good again. Hallie thought he would be the perfect sex partner. She knew he wouldn't turn her down. They kept their affair a secret. At first, they hooked up two or three times a week. Then their liaisons slacked off to twice a month.

One night, When Jackie walked Gerald to the door, she saw Ron going into Hallie's back door. She watched as her son's girlfriend greeted Ron naked. It wasn't a surprise that Hallie was sleeping around, but with Jamal's best friend—that was a shocker. Jackie had given up on the idea that she would break Jamal and Hallie up. She had to face it. She had a weak son. She believed telling him this wouldn't make any difference. So she wasn't going to waste her time telling him.

Weeks went by, and Ron's test results came back. He had long since moved out again and couldn't be found. Jackie still carried a lot of compassion for Ron, and she wasn't going to let anyone stand in the way of that.

Jamal was coming home for Travis and Randy's graduation.

Kathy's jealousy over Gerald was making her despise Jackie. She started to befriend Hallie just to have an allied against Jackie. Neither was woman enough to face Jackie head-on. The pair gossiped and spread lies about Jackie.

Jackie didn't know Kathy had turned against her. She thought Kathy was still her best friend, but she saw less of Kathy as time went by.

Days, weeks, and months went by quickly. Jamal called; he was coming home, and the wedding was back on. Hallie had been preparing for it for months. He took some extra time off for their honeymoon that he had planned in Hawaii. He wanted the trip to be a surprise.

Hallie was smirking because she had won. The wedding was on. She had gotten her man, and there was nothing Jackie could do about it. Her suitcases were packed. Invitations were mailed out. She had a beautiful wedding gown. She was finally getting out of the projects. She couldn't wait to leave.

Jackie was desperate. She had to make sure that when Jamal came home, he didn't have sex with Hallie. Jackie had kept this secret for so long. Now she had to take matters into her own hands. Time was narrowing down. She had no plan.

In the meantime she thought she could trust Kathy enough to share her problem with her. She shared what she knew about Hallie and Ron.

Kathy, in return, let Hallie know Jackie had plans to break them up.

"If that bitch wants a war," Hallie told Kathy, "then it's on. I don't care if she's Jamal's mom. I will beat her old ass. Jamal doesn't care too much for her anyway. He told me he was getting tired of her sticking her nose in our business. You know what? Don't tell me anything else that bitch said. You just as dirty as she is."

Kathy was stunned that Hallie had turned on her. Hallie believe in speaking her mine. She considered no one a friend who hung around Jackie.

Kathy was so pissed off with Hallie that she started talking against Hallie to Jackie. "You know, I've seen guys going in Hallie's apartment late at night. She is a whore. I wouldn't be surprised if Gerald was messing with her."

"She's too young for Gerald," Jackie replied. "I'm going to tell you something that you can't tell anyone."

"Okay, I won't tell anyone. I promise. Besides," Kathy added, "who would I tell? You're the only one I talk to."

"I told you about Hallie and Ron," Jackie started, "but what I didn't tell you was that I took Ron to the clinic. He tested positive for HIV. No one knows this but him and I and now you. So I better not hear of this from anyone else."

"I promise," Kathy swore. "I'm so glad Michelle is not here. Oh my God, now I know I did the right thing by sending her away."

Jackie looked at Kathy in disagreement but kept silent. "I have to make sure Jamal and Hallie don't hook up."

"How are you going to do that?" Kathy asked. "You know how he feels about her. He knows she cheats and he still messes with her."

"I know," Jackie said. "I have to come up with something fast."

"Blackmail her," Kathy suggested. "Tell her she's HIV positive and you're going to tell everybody. You know how she is. She's more concerned about what people think about her than anything else."

"No, I wouldn't do something like that to my worst enemy."

"She is your worst enemy."

"My point exactly. Not only would that ruin her," Jackie added, "but it would hurt Ron too. I won't do that. But what I will do is let her know that I know about her and Ron and that she'd better tell Jamal before I do."

"I hate to call you stupid," Kathy replied, "but you are if you think that's going to work. Once they are alone, you know what's going to happen."

"That's why I'm going to tell him about Ron first, and I'm going to pretend that I'm letting her tell him. I know how dirty Hallie is. I have to tell him about Ron testing positive for HIV to make sure he doesn't have sex with her. If this doesn't break them up, then he deserves whatever she puts him through. I'll give up. I will never have anything to do with him because I won't be able to face the idea that I raised a weak son."

"It's pitiful," Kathy agreed. "We do the best we can to raise them, and they think they know more than us. We're just trying to protect them from being hurt. They think they know everything since they're having sex. Since when does sex make you smart?"

"It doesn't. It makes some people act like fools."

"For Jamal's sake and yours I hope he listens to you this time."

Jackie nodded in agreement. "I'm glad Travis isn't like Jamal. Travis is going into the air force. He's already talked with a recruiter. So right after graduation, he's leaving. Both my babies will be gone."

"I guess Randy will be leaving for college?"

"Yeah, he's gotten several scholarships. He's going to college. Then he wants play pro football. He's just as good as Ron."

Kathy drew in her breath. "I hope he's smarter than Ron. I can't believe Ron walked away from all that money. That was stupid."

"He could have had it all," Jackie agreed. "Sad, so sad. Of all people, he was who I was praying would make it, just to show Vera."

"Believe it or not, I was too. I wanted him to succeed for that same reason. Have you heard from Vera?"

Jackie shook her head. "No one has seen or heard from her, and I wasn't expecting to."

*　　*　　*

The next day, Jackie let Hallie know that she knew about her and Ron. Jackie told Hallie she wanted her to tell Jamal that she had slept with Ron. Jackie also told Hallie to end it for good with Jamal. Jackie didn't mention Ron's test results.

Hallie was furious. "He's not going to believe you!" she yelled, narrowing her eyes. "Even if he did, there's nothing you can tell him that will break us up. I got your son, sweetie, wrapped around my you know what. Get used to it, bitch. Go ahead and tell him. It won't break us up. You have a weak, dumbass son. Look at how many times you've stuck your nose in our business, and he came back to me. I don't care what you tell him." She hung up the phone.

"Whoooooo! That witch." Jackie was at her wits' end. The only thing left was to pray—something she hadn't been doing much of lately. "Dear

God," she began. "I'm so sorry for praying only when I need you. Forgive me for messing with a married man. I promise I'll give that part of my life up. I need you to please protect my son. Please, please, give him wisdom to see things for what they really are. If anyone needs to be punished, let it be me. God, please don't let my son end up with Hallie. Please let him see her for what she is before it's too late. God, I pray to you with all my heart. Protect my son and look out for Ron too. I pray to you, almighty. Amen."

Jackie got off her knees and called Kathy to share her ordeal about Hallie.

"You better make sure they're never alone together," Kathy warned. "I told you what to do and you refused. That's probably where Jamal got his weakness from."

Jackie didn't like Kathy saying that, but she was right. Jackie blamed herself for her son's weakness. She wished her sons had had a man around to help raise them. Maybe Jamal wouldn't be having these problems if he'd had a strong male role model. In this day and age, you had to do the best you could by yourself.

Jackie was on edge and nervous about Jamal's homecoming. Everyone was happy to see him. Ron was no where around. Jackie had a small gathering for Travis and Randy's graduation. Randy and Travis kept Jamal busy. They were glad to see him. Jackie had told Randy and Travis about Hallie's cheating, telling them to make sure they keep Jamal away from Hallie.

Hallie—by court order—was not allowed to set foot in Jackie's apartment. But that didn't stop her from calling every ten to fifteen minutes.

Jamal was so excited about seeing his family and some familiar faces that he didn't rush to Hallie. He told his mother in private his little secret. "Mom, I met this nice young lady. She's totally the opposite of Hallie. I remember what you said. I will know the difference between lust and love. I met someone who understands me. She doesn't like to argue or fight. She treats me like she appreciates me. Mom, now I know what it's like to be loved. You were right. I confused lust with love. For the first time, I can say that I'm truly in love. Hallie had this power over me, but not anymore."

"Are you serious?" Jackie asked.

"I'd better be," Jamal said. "We're married and expecting a baby."

"What!" Jackie exclaimed excitedly. "When?! Oh my God! Are you for real? I'm going to be a grandma. Thank you God."

"Yeah, I'm so happy. I love her. I really love her, and she loves me. The baby's due in four months. If it's a girl, we're going to name her after you, a boy after Daddy."

"What about Hallie?" Jackie asked. "Have you told her?"

Jamal shook his head. "I'm having a good time being with you guys. I'll break the news on the day that I'm leaving. I'm not up for all that drama she creates."

"How are you going to break it to her?"

Jamal shrugged. "I'm just going to tell her it's time to move on. That's all. I don't want to rub salt in her wound. You understand, Mom. I got my sensitive side from you."

"Well I guess I did do a good job raising you boys." Jackie smiled. "There's nothing wrong with a sensitive man."

Jamal grinned. "Mom, you did a great job with us. Never doubt yourself. We may not be doctors or lawyers, but we're not on drugs, in gangs, or in jail. So never doubt yourself. I think we turned out right. I love you, Mom." Jamal gave his mom a kiss on the cheek

Jackie hugged Jamal. "I'm so proud of you, my son." She lowered her voice to a whisper. "Thank you, God."

Jamal made sure he stayed away from Hallie until it was time to leave. He didn't want any confrontation.

Hallie was becoming desperate. She went to Jackie's apartment. Jackie had started keeping the door locked so Hallie wouldn't just walk in. Hallie felt that, if she could get Jamal alone, she could seduce him and get him back on track. If he could see her in her hot pink nightie—that piece of lingerie had always made him go wild. She noticed he was avoiding her..

Hallie was too presumptuous. She would do whatever it took to get Jamal in her bed. "Jamal!" She yelled as loudly as she could as she banged on the door, "Jamal, Jamal! I know you're in there. Come out, you coward. Why are you avoiding me?"

"Get away from my door before I call the police," Jackie called.

Hallie kept knocking.

"I got this, Mom," Jamal said. "Go get the car so you can take me to the airport, We can grab something to eat there."

Jamal went out and walked past Hallie so she would follow him. He was getting her away from his mother. There was so much tension between Hallie and Jackie that it was just a matter of time before one of them struck the other.

Hallie followed, talking as she walked. "Why are you avoiding me? You've been here for a full week and have not spent any time with me." She looked at Jackie sitting in the car watching them.

Jackie was ready to defend her son if Hallie did something irrational.

"I'm not riding with your mother," Hallie said. "We can take a cab." She tried to put her arm around Jamal, but he pulled away. "What's wrong, baby?"

"You and me—that's what's wrong. I can't pretend that everything is cool between us."

"What are you trying to say?" Hallie asked.

"It's over," Jamal said.

"What did I do? You promised me you would take me away from all this."

"That's it," Jamal replied. "You never loved me, and you made sure our friends and my family knew it. I was your ticket out of the projects. You were using me. I know once I'd gotten you out of here, you would have eventually dumped me for someone better."

"How can you think like that?" Hallie asked. "I have sent out wedding invitations, and my bags are packed. You can't call the whole thing off. What will our friends think?"

"You know what they will think," Jamal said. "It's about time that I came to my senses. All your friends—that's right, your friends as well as mine—said you were fooling around on me, and I surely don't want a woman I can't trust and who doesn't respect my mom.

"It's done, Hallie," Jamal said, his tone turning gentle. "I hope you find your ticket out." He turned to walk away.

"No, please don't leave me here," she cried out. "Please don't leave me." She dropped to her knees and grabbed hold of one of Jamal's legs. "Please take me with you. Please don't leave me here," she sobbed.

Jamal kept walking without looking at her. "Don't do this," he said. "Don't make a scene. It will only embarrass you. You carried yourself as the one with authority in this relationship, so don't humble yourself now. It's so not you. Your friends are staring. Don't let them see this side of you. They will mock you. Get up." He lifts her up.

So she stood there facing him, tears rolling down her eyes. She composed herself. Out of fear, she begged him to take her with him. She would change. The promises came way too late for Jamal.

"What's going to happen to me?" she asked. "Who's going to take care of me?"

Jamal didn't answer. He got in the car.

Hallie was left standing there watching the car drive off. "Who's going to take care of me?" She yell out repeatedly untill the car had disappeared.

For the first time, Hallie was embarrassed to face her friends. She isolated herself in her room. Days turned into weeks, and weeks into months. She brainwashed herself into believing she and Jamal would get back together. She was sure Jamal would come back to her, begging as always. When he didn't return her calls, realization set in. She would never hear from Jamal again.

As Hallie grew more and more depressed, Kathy became manipulative. She took this opportunity to feed Hallie information. She told Hallie that Jamal was married and expecting a baby, and that Jackie had introduced the couple to each other. Hallie was angry enough to want to kill Jackie, which was exactly what Kathy had planned; she hoped Hallie would do some physical harm to Jackie.

"You ought to tell Gerald's wife Jackie is messing with her husband," Kathy suggested.

Hallie knew what Kathy was trying to do. She had seen Gerald sneak in and out of Kathy's apartment as well.

Every day, Kathy would call Hallie to gossip about Jackie. She would lie and tell her things Jackie said about her.

Hallie didn't like Jackie, but she also didn't like two-faced people. She let Kathy know in no uncertain terms. Kathy got the message. She felt she had succeeded in her mission anyway. She didn't need to feed Hallie any more information. Hallie was sitting in her apartment doing a lot of thinking. Her hatred for Jackie was building up inside her.

One day, Jackie and Kathy were sitting on the porch laughing and making conversation when Hallie went to the mailbox. She assumed that Jackie and Kathy was laughing and mocking her. Hallie went inside, her hate and rage growing, nearing boiling point. She had always wanted to kick Jackie's ass, but she hadn't been able to because she was going with Jackie's son. But nothing was stopping her now. She had nothing to lose. She put on some old clothes to fight in.

Kathy and Jackie saw her coming. They knew she was coming for trouble.

"Don't come over here to start anything," Jackie warned.

Hallie reached Jackie's porch. Pointing her finger in Jackie's face, she moved closer toward Jackie. Kathy moved aside so she wouldn't accidently get hit.

"You meddling bitch," Hallie snarled. "You think you won. Well I got something for you."

Jackie pushed Hallie's hand away, but Hallie put it back in Jackie's face.

"Get your hand out of my face," Jackie said evenly.

"Make me, bitch," Hallie said, daring Jackie. "I want you to do something. I will kick your ass all over this place."

Jackie rose from her seat. "Get off my porch," she demanded, repeating herself when Hallie didn't budge.

Kathy giggled, wanting Jackie to get beaten down knowing Jackie was no match for Hallie's youth.

All the yelling, screaming, and cussing brought everyone in hearing range to Jackie's yard. Word got out that Miss Jackie and Hallie were about to throw down. People came running just to see. This was going to be one of those fights everyone would be discussing again and again. The yard and the street were full. Everyone was trying to see.

Jackie kept telling Hallie to get off her porch. Hallie was inviting Jackie off the porch.

"You weren't satisfied until you broke us up," Hallie said bitterly. "Everyone knew you wanted Jamal for yourself. That's right, bitch, you were screwing your own son. You freak."

"You're a dumb whore," Jackie replied. "I'm not going to dignify that ridiculous accusation. "You're just mad because Jamal dumped you."

Hallie got back in Jackie's face. "He didn't dump me," she snarled. "You interfered in our relationship. If it wasn't for you, we would still be together. You old slut."

"Get off my porch," Jackie said firmly.

The tension was heating up.

"Bitch!" Hallie screamed. "Move me, bitch!"

"This is what I'm talking about," Jackie replied. "Look at you. I'm glad my son found a beautiful, caring woman who loves him and that they are married and expecting a baby! I'm so glad he didn't get stuck with a lowlife like you. I'm thrilled to death over my new daughter-in-law."

Hallie slapped Jackie as hard as she could. The move came as a surprise, and before Jackie could react, Hallie had flown back to her own yard. Jackie was furious that Hallie had run before she could strike back. The slap was so loud that people gasped for their own breaths, as if it was one of them who had gotten hit.

Jackie was going to get even, and the only way to hurt Hallie was verbally. Jackie was going to make sure everyone heard what she had to say. She was mad as hell. This witch had put her hand in her face. . "You better take your skinny ass home," Jackie yelled. You want to know why I kept my son from your whorest ass. Everyone knows you will screw anything. You even messed with Jamal's best friend, Ron. Did you know Ron has AIDS? Now who's the slut? That's why I didn't want my son messing with you anymore. Go get tested, you whore!"

All eyes were on Hallie, who was speechless. This time, she was lost for words. She saw Kathy's smirk on her face. Hallie couldn't believe Jackie would strike below the belt like that. *None of it is true*, she told herself. *It can't be. Jackie's lying to embarrass me.*

Hallie looked at Kathy, who was enjoying herself too much. Hallie had to have the last word in this fight. So she directed her rage at Kathy. "What the hell you laughing at, Kathy? Did you tell your best friend that you're both screwing the same man and you're stupid enough to get pregnant by him?"

Kathy was shocked that Hallie had blurted her secret out. Baker Street was getting its share of drama today.

Jackie looked at Kathy's stomach. Her belly was extended.

"That's right," Hallie continued, "you both screwing a married man who don't want neither one of you bitches. He leaves one to go screw the other, all in the same night—not to mention the other damn women he's messing with. Who need the AIDS test now? Y'all sharing the same man. How nasty is that? Fuck all you bitches!"

Now the crowd was staring at Jackie and Kathy. Hallie was proud of herself. Her fight was done. She declared victory, turned, and went inside.

Hallie was afraid people might believe what Jackie had said and that rumors would spread about her. She could lose her popularity. "Oh please don't let this be true," Hallie whispered. "I don't want people treating me like I'm contagious."

Back on Jackie's porch, Jackie asked Kathy, "Are you pregnant by Gerald?"

"Uh-huh, yeah," she muttered. "So what, You don't own him." Kathy was glad it was out in the open. She didn't have to hide her feelings anymore.

Jackie was hurt. "Get the hell off my porch, you backstabbing whore," she yelled. "How could you call yourself my friend? Is this how you treat your friends? I trusted you. Get the hell out of my sight."

Kathy left quickly. She didn't want anything to hurt her unborn baby—the baby she believed would bring her and Gerald together. She was going to tell him tonight about her pregnancy. She didn't have to worry about Jackie being with Gerald anymore.

Jackie went inside, feeling hurt, angry, and betrayed. She'd been hurt by her lover, she was angry that she had stooped to Hallie's level, and her best friend had betrayed her.

Kathy was please with herself. She felt she finally got Jackie out of Gerald's life.

Hallie was scared and worried. Had Ron had AIDS while they were having sex? Had he known he was infected? *Oh my gosh, I have to get tested.*

Months went by. Hallie stayed confined in her house. She didn't talk to any of her friends. Her mother assumed her depression was over her breakup with Jamal still.

No one saw much of Jackie or Kathy anymore. They never spoke to each other again after Jackie discovered that Kathy was involved with Gerald.

Kathy told Gerald she was pregnant. She didn't get the response she was looking for. He gave her money for an abortion. She didn't have it. He left her alone after that. He never spoke to her again. He denied the baby was his and threatened to kill Kathy if she told his wife her lie. Kathy took Gerald's rejection hard.

Jackie was done with him. She realized getting involved with a married man was a mistake, and she realized that you can't share all your secrets with your best friend. She remembered telling her sons about moral values. She wished now that she had listened to her own advice. She couldn't believe she'd been messing with this whorest man and never was using protection.

Jackie decided to get tested for AIDS. Jackie made a promise to God that if it came back negative, she would never commit adultery again.

Rumors were circulating—Hallie had AIDS, and Jackie and Kathy were pregnant by the same married man. The gossip that was spreading was half truth and half lies.

Jackie's test came back negative. She was done with sex.

Kathy couldn't let go of Gerald. She called him all the time and followed him whenever she could. Crying often and stressing herself out which made her go into labor early. Her daughter weighed four pounds and two ounces. She was in an incubator for months. Gerald didn't call or come to see them.

Part III

The Future

Chapter sixteen

What happens now?

Kathy had no money, no job, and no friends. She had to apply for food stamps and governments check. Kathy found out other women had claimed to be pregnant by or have had a baby with Gerald. And he didn't claim any of them.

Kathy needed money to buy her child some food. She went to Gerald's house while his wife wasn't home. When he saw her at his door, he got his shotgun. She was crying and holding her daughter. She was hoping that once he saw their daughter, he would fall in love with her.

"What the hell you doing showing up here?" Gerald demanded.

"I brought your daughter so you could see her," Kathy said.

"That's not my child," Gerald growled. ". Get the hell off my property before I blow your brains out!" He pointed the shotgun at her.

"Please," Kathy stuttered, "I—I—I need money to buy your daughter some food. We don't have any food or money."

"That's not my problem," Gerald replied coolly. "Get the hell away from here before my wife comes home. I told you when you took it upon yourself to have that damn thing not to get any ideals. This is your problem, not mine. When I leave and come back, you better be gone." Gerald slammed the door in Kathy's face.

Kathy didn't have anyone to turn to. She tried to call Michelle, but Michelle was still refusing her calls. The only way she got through one day was by telling Michelle's secretary to tell her that Ron was sick.

Michelle took the call.

"Michelle, this is your mother."

"I know who you are," Michelle replied. "You don't have to remind me. What's wrong with Ron?" Concern was clear in her voice as she asked this.

"He's dying," Kathy told her. "He has AIDS."

Michelle got quiet. She stood there holding the phone next to her chest as tears flowed down her face.

"Michelle," Kathy said. "Michelle, are you still there?"

Hearing Kathy's voice snapped Michelle out of her daze.

"Can you send me some money?" Kathy asked. "I need to buy your sister and I some food, we have nothing to eat."

Michelle was furious. "How dare you ask me for money? You killed my baby! You ripped my baby from my wound. You knew I wanted my baby. Now you want me to support yours. I hate you. You didn't abort yours. Remember what you told me—I couldn't afford to have a baby. You should have taken your own advice."

"Please don't hate your sister," Kathy begged. "We have no food. You're the only one I can ask. I have no one. If you deny me, what will I do?"

"Put the baby up for adoption," Michelle replied coldly. "You can't support her, so get rid of her—like you did mine." Michelle didn't feel like talking anymore, so she placed the receiver in its cradle.

She told her secretary to book her a flight to Greensboro, North Carolina ASAP.

Michelle was the youngest pediatrician in the world and the smartest. She was responsible for medical breakthroughs in children's care. She had written two number-one, best-selling medical books. She was still taking classes and top in her field. She was in high demand, but she wanted to be there for Ron. Her feelings for Ron have never left her.

*   *   *

Hallie's results came back. On this sunny, beautiful morning, the sounds of kids playing or loud music were absent. The quietness was too good to last long. The doors and windows were open to catch the outside breeze. Suddenly, a faint sound of sirens pierced the silence, growing louder . It came to a stop, as flashing lights lit up Baker Street.

Jackie heard screams and cries. She got up to see what was going on outside.

Victoria was crying. "Not my baby," she screamed. "Oh God, please not my baby."

People were running out of their apartments to see what was happening. Jackie stood in the doorway trying to hear what was going on. She saw Hallie being carried out on a stretcher and Victoria getting in the back of the ambulance. Jackie watch as it carried them away, sirens blaring.

Rumors were already spreading—Hallie had died on the way to the hospital. She died at the hospital. She died from AIDS.

In truth, Victoria had found Hallie dead in her bedroom. Hallie had written two suicide notes.

The first read:

Dear Mother,

I'm so sorry for hurting you. Please don't be embarrassed or disappointed in me. I love you, Mother. It's nothing you did. It's just that I can't and won't live like this. The shame of everyone knowing and distancing themselves—it's an outcome I won't live with. The decision to do this was easy. The how was the hardest. I wanted to cut my wrist, but I didn't want you to touch my contaminate blood. I am going to miss you, Mom. I hope you find a way out. Go back into modeling. You're still so beautiful. Give this sealed letter to Jackie please. I love you, mom.

At the funeral, Victoria gave Jackie Hallie's sealed letter. The letter read:

I'm so sorry for disrespecting you. I love you, Ms. Jackie. I'm just sad I didn't realize this sooner. You were right to protect your son from someone like me, and Jamal made the right decision. I'm so sorry for what I put you both through. Please forgive me.

Jackie kept reading the letter over and over again. She blamed herself for Hallie's death. She would never be quite the same.

Jamal came home to attend the funeral.

Jackie started gaining weight. She overate as a product of depression and loneliness. Travis was away in the military. Randy was in college and playing college football. Randy didn't know his brother had AIDS, and Jackie hadn't told him. Ron stayed hidden in his rooming house.

Randy and Jamal visited him there. They saw how he had deteriorated. Randy was angry with Ron. "How could you be so stupid?" he challenged. "I hate you. Look at you. You let us down. You let me down. Vera was right about you. We had a plan, you and I. We're all we got now, and you got to go off and get AIDS." Randy slammed the door after he walked out.

Jackie heard about Randy's nasty visit with his brother. "Randy, you should never ever talk to your brother like that," she scolded. "You told him you hated him. How could you?"

"He let me down," Randy said. "We were to be here for each other. We were to do everything together. He went and got himself sick. He proved Vera right."

"Then you prove her wrong," Jackie said firmly. "You make your brother proud. Go back over there and make amends before it's too late. You're all he has as a blood relative here. Don't let him die believing you hate him too."

Randy knew he had been wrong. He went back and apologized to Ron. "Hey, bro," he said softly, "I'm sorry. I didn't mean any of those things I said. I just don't want to lose you. You're all I got. I love you, man." Tears swelling in his eyes, Randy gave Ron a hug. Randy wished at that moment that he could turn back time.

Then it occurred to him—*Turn it back to what?* They had never had a happy time in their life.

Ron was pushing back from Randy. The embrace was beginning to hurt him. "Hey, man, it's going to be all right," he said. "I was reckless. I was trying to self-destruct. I've been experiencing hurt and pain all my life. I just wanted the ultimate pain, so I wouldn't have to feel it anymore. You—you're different than me. You're the strong one. Don't be a failure. You're a man now. Go and make our dreams come true."

"Our dream will come to life," Randy said with conviction. "You can help me."

"Don't let anyone steal your glory," Ron told his brother. "When agents come to the games, all the players start showing off."

"You know everything." Randy grabbed Ron and pulls him close so he could give him one more embrace, afraid it may be their last.

They both said how much they loved each other.

"Make me proud, little bro," Ron said. Ron got up and started walking toward the door hoping Randy would follow.

Randy was not ready to say good-bye. "When I sign my NFL contracts and buy that mansion, you're staying with me," Randy said. "We're going to travel all over the world together. So hang in there. It's going to be you and me hanging out like old times. You're going to get the best care money can buy. I'm going to take good care of you. Just wait and see."

Ron motioned Randy to the door. He was ready to rest. This had been a long, emotional visit.

After Randy left, he said a silent prayer. He talked to his god as if he was there in the flesh. "God, what did we do to deserve this? A mother who didn't give a damn and our dads who didn't care enough to protect us. We were just innocent children. Why didn't you protect us? My brother doesn't deserve any more suffering. Give his suffering to me instead. Let my brother have some happiness before he dies. I pray to you with all my heart and soul. Amen."

*　　*　　*

Michelle secretively came into town. She didn't want her mother to know she was there. She still hadn't forgiven Kathy.

She saw the condition Ron was living in. She wanted him to live comfortably. She leased a two-bedroom condo for them. Ron tried to reject Michelle, but he was too weak. He was in a wheelchair by this point. She put him on new AIDS medication and bought new clothes for him.

Ron refused to talk to Michelle. He was mad at her for taking over his life without asking him.

Michelle blamed her mother for Ron's downfall. She was determined to get him back on his feet—to make him well again. While taking care of Ron she realized her feelings for him still ran deep. She bathed him, fed him, and made him take his meds.

Soon, he got his strength back and was looking better. He gained some of his weight back and was looking like his old self. Once he was strong, he told Michelle she shouldn't be there. He tried to refuse any more of her assistance and care. She told him that she was glad to be there for him.

The pair took a trip down memory lane, and Michelle apologized about the abortion. He told her how that day had changed his life forever—he had stopped caring about anything after that day. Michelle told Ron that she had never stopped loving him and she wanted to be his wife. He was shocked to hear this. Ron believed he wasn't good enough for Michelle. He told her no. She explained that the marriage would give her rights as his wife that could benefit him. Ron continues refusing Michelle proposal. He would only said yes if Michelle promise that she would agree the marriage was only for medical reason and there be no sex; only then would he agree.

They were married by a justice of the peace. Michelle took Ron to the Virgin Islands. She made sure he had everything he needed. Since learning about Ron's illness, she had start researching and working to find a cure for AIDS. Michelle was desperate to find a cure quickly. She worked religiously.

"I told everyone you were going to be fine as hell when you grew up," Ron said with a smile.

"Ooh, so you're saying," Michelle teased. "I was an ugly little girl."

"No," Ron protested, "that's not what I thought. I liked you."

"You ran from me. I had this unbelievable crush on you. Here I was, this ugly, little girl, wanting the most handsome man on the universe to want me. What was I thinking?" She laughed out loud.

"Look at you now," Ron said. "You're not going to have a problem getting a man now. Anyone would be a fool to reject you."

Michelle playfully sprinkled water on him. Ron grabbed her arm as he put his hand under the running water and returned the gesture. They both played until they were all wet. They laughed until Michelle turned serious.

"Why didn't you return my letters or my calls?" she asked.

"What letters? I never received any letters, and you know when Mom left our phone was disconnected. I assumed you were like the rest of the girls I'd been with until Ms. Jackie explained to me you were too young to make your own decisions. You had no say-so about your life or our baby. I should have known better. I heard the abortion was just as hard on you as it was on me."

Michelle's eyes got misty. "I wanted our baby so much. I will never forgive my mother."

"Do me a favor, Michelle," Ron said gently. "Don't carry this grudge against your mother any longer. She was doing what she felt was right. It's time for you to do what's right."

Michelle tried to change the subject.

"You are stubborn," Ron pressed. "But I'm serious, Michelle. Make peace with yourself so you can make amends with your mother."

Michelle started caressing Ron's back and chest. She wanted Ron to make love to her, but he kept refusing her. He push her away

"I told you," Ron said. "Don't even think about us getting together like that."

"We can make love," Michelle told him. "People with AIDS do it all the time with protection."

"I'm not going to take a chance with your life."

"Look, Ron, who's the doctor here? I know how to protect myself."

"What's really going on here, Michelle? Are you trying to fulfill a childhood dream? Or are you still getting even with your mother?"

"I want to make you happy," She said.

"You can't say you're doing this for me," he protested. "This isn't making me happy. It hurts to have you here. I'm afraid to hold you or kiss you—to love you. Just having you here brings back painful memories. I'm crying more now since you've been back in my life. Why are you here—to pay me back for hurting you? I think it's time for us to say good-bye."

"I never stopped loving you," Michelle replied. "I saved myself just to be with you again. No other man can touch my heart the way you did. You say it hurts to have me around. Well it hurts me when you're not around. You complete me. I don't want anyone else in my life but you."

"You haven't experienced life yet. To say I complete you is preemptive."

"Ron, let me please you. I need you now. I promise I know what I'm doing. I have three best-selling medical books. I'm a scientist of medicine. I am a doctor, and the doctor needs a little taking care of right now," she said, her tone turning seductive. "No one can tell us what to do anymore. Please make love to me. I need you now."Michelle undressed slowly in front of Ron and stood there naked.

He couldn't believe how beautiful she looked. She had filled out in all the right places. Ron didn't need his wheelchair anymore—he had regained his strength—but he almost lost his balance staring at Michelle's naked body. He felt the hardness grow in his pants. It had been years since he'd had a woman. "This is not fair to me," he protested.

Michelle gave Ron the condom.

"I'm scared. I don't think this is a good idea."

"Don't think. Just shut up and make love to me. Remember the promise you made to me. You said you would never hurt me again. You know if you reject me that will hurt me."

Ron had to admit Michelle had a way of getting what she wanted when she wanted it. He finally gave in to her advances.

Ron looked and felt like a healthy man again. While on the islands, women were coming on to Ron. Michelle found it to be a turn on as long as it wasn't physical

While lying in bed after making love, Michelle asked Ron, "If you could go back in time, where would you go and why?"

"I would go back to where I met you. I would wait until you were older. I would save myself for you. You taught me the meaning of love and how to love. I asked god to let me know what love is. Now I know. I wish I had done things differently." Lying in Michelle's lap, Ron stop breathing.

Michelle knew the unthinkable had just happened. She felt it. "Ron! Wake up, my love. Ron, oh my love. Don't leave me. Don't leave me now." She kissed his face and sobbed. "I'm not ready to let you go. I will always love you. It's not fair. We just found each other again.

"I'm going to miss you, my love," she whispered."Ron death was sudden and unexpected. He was doing so well on the new medications.It will take an autopsy to determine the exact cause of his death.

She lay there all night, holding Ron in her arms and sobbing. The next day Michelle made arrangements to fly Ron's body back to North Carolina. Michelle had a small memorial with friends and Randy. Kathy was not allowed at the funeral. No one expected Vera to show, so it was no surprise when she didn't. Michelle, as Ron's wife was in charge of all his arrangements. She had him cremated.

She had his ashes condensed in to a small locket so she could keep him close to her heart always. She would never take the locket off.

Once the service was over, Michelle caught the first flight out of North Carolina. Ron's death made Michelle resent her mother even more. If her mother would have stayed out of their business, he would still be alive today. They would have been married and happy, raising their kids and traveling. Life would have been good. Instead, Kathy had killed their baby, their dream, their happiness, and now, her husband.

As she boarded the plane, she grasped the locket. Once seated, she closed her eyes so she could visualize every moment of her and Ron's time together. She was more determined to find a cure for AIDS.

She set up a foundation called Ron's Love Foundation. All her memories about their love for each other she put into a book. It was translated into seven different languages, and it was on *The New York* Times Best Sellers' list. All the proceeds from the book went to Ron's Love Foundations.

Their story was made into a motion picture. It was a hit at the box office. Not a dry eye came out of the theater. The title of the movie was *Till Death Do Us Part.*

Michelle worked relentlessly working on a cure for AIDS. She spent all her time working, traveling, and giving speeches. Michelle's books and journals and her medical practice made her a multimillionaire.

Randy also took Ron's death hard. With his brother gone, he was all alone. He applied his frustrations in his sports, which made him the all-time favorite in college football.

Randy would eventually become a wide receiver for the Tennessee Lions and would lead his team to the Super Bowl twice, where the Lions would win both times. He would get several endorsements and commercials and TV offers.

He would buy Jackie a five-bedroom, two and half-bathroom house in a nice, quiet, upscale neighborhood.

* * *

Jackie lived in the home Randy had bought for her by herself. Jamal and Travis both lived in different states. They were both still in the military. Jamal and his wife had three kids. He rarely visited, but he called once a month. Travis called every day and visited every chance he got. He was still single.

Randy took care of Jackie's living expenses and got her a new Mercedes. At the beginning Jackie flew out to all of Randy's games he would introduced her to his friends and coaches as Mom.

Jackie had no friends. The neighbors lived miles apart from each other. No one visited or sat on the porch. She never saw kids playing outside.

Jackie fed her lonesomeness by overeating and junk food. She wasn't active anymore. She spent her time watching TV. She became overweight and was taking medication for high blood pressure and diabetes. This once active, beautiful, young-looking woman now looked older than her age. Jackie was also taking medication for depression. She still blamed herself for Hallie's death.

*   *   *

Michelle discovered how the AIDS virus enter the target cell. She would soon make a vaccination that would stop the spread of the virus. This was a major medical breakthrough.

For Michelle, it wasn't enough. She wanted to discover a cure. She worked diligently. She had written more medical journals and had won two Biotech awards; this was the highest medical award given in the world. She traveled all over the world giving speeches and appearing on talk shows. She was featured on magazine covers and soon had made appearances on all the major world news channels. Glamour Girl magazine voted Michelle the sexiest medical scientist in the United States. Michelle was worth around six hundred million dollars.

On one of Michelle's business trips she met Brad. Brad was a corporate attorney. He was a billionaire, Caucasian, and attractive. Michelle was on her way to Atlanta to give a speech. People recognized her everywhere she went. Brad and Michelle met on her flight to Atlanta.

For Brad, it was love at first sight. Michelle was not interested. Brad pursued Michelle until she finally said yes to a date.

After a year of dating, they were married. She still harbored feelings for Ron. She couldn't give Brad the love he deserved, and he knew why. He read her autobiography, Till *Death Do Us Part*. Michelle felt guilty for being with Brad. She had made it clear to him before they were married that she was not in love with him, though she cares for him. Theirs was a one-sided relationship.

Michelle started extending her business trips to avoid coming home to Brad. She told Brad that, if he wanted a divorce, she wouldn't contest it.

Brad wouldn't hear of it. He thought Michelle would eventually fall in love with him. He loved her unconditionally.

Brad tried to make peace between Michelle and her mother. Without letting Michelle know, he was sending a check to Kathy. Michelle wouldn't appreciate his doing so. If she were to find out, it could be the end of their marriage.

Brad was a patient man. He had to be. He endured seeing Ron's locket around his wife's neck every day. Even during lovemaking she refused to take it off. Michelle believed she was protecting Ron. Brad needed to know how to compete with someone who no longer exist. How could he win Michelle's heart?

Brad was fifteen years older than Michelle, and he was beginning to feel more like a protective father than her husband.

One evening, Kathy called, and Michelle answered. Kathy asked Michelle if she and her daughter could move in with her and Brad. The Hamptons was getting to dangerous to live in. They couldn't sit on the porch; nor could her child play outside. Kathy's apartment had been broken into several times. The thieves had stolen the TV, clothes, and the toaster. Kathy was afraid to live there.

Michelle's hatred for her mother had grown deeper over the years. "How dare you call here?" she snapped. "I don't want you in the same state I'm in. You need help, go ask Jackie for forgiveness. You're good at hurting people for your own self-preservation. Stay out of my life. I don't care what happens to you or your child. You didn't care about my baby. Why should I care about yours?

"I hate you," she screamed into the phone. "You ripped my baby from my womb—my baby! My baby! I wanted my baby!"! Michelle's anger had come to the surface, and she couldn't stop herself. "You are a dirty, backstabbing, two-faced bitch. Look what you did to Ron, to my baby, and to the only real friend you ever had. Jackie was a good friend to you. She would do anything for you. Go ask Jackie for help. She will forgive you, but I won't. I will never forgive you for what you did to me and my baby. I hate your guts."

Kathy was crying. "I'm sorry. I'm so sorry," she said over and over. "I believed I was doing the right thing. I didn't know it would hurt ..."

Brad heard his wife histrionic behavior. He ran to her rescue, taking the phone and consoling her. He held Michelle tightly as she cried her heart out.

Placing the phone to his ear, he said quietly, "This not a good time." He hung up. Picking Michelle up, he carried her to her bedroom, took off her shoes, and covered her with a bedspread. He sat on the side of Michelle's bed stroking her hair as he talk.

Michelle was still emotionally distraught.

"Honey, you can't keep letting yourself get upset like this," Brad said. "You have to let go and forgive. We can go together for professional counseling. We can't keep living like this, Michelle. We're sleeping in separate rooms. You're always out of town on business trips. You're hardly home anymore, and when you are, we don't act like husband and wife. I don't know what we have here. You know how much I love you. But you have to get some help."

"I'm a medical doctor. I'm a scientist. I have a degree in psychology. I have found cures for diseases. I have written best-selling books. What can be wrong with me? I'm not the one who needs help. My purpose in life is to help others. I don't need help," Michelle gasped. She grabbed her locket and brought it to her lips.

Sitting on the edge of Michelle's bed, Brad watched her kiss the locket. She turned away from him, and he heard her whisper, "I will never let anyone tear us apart again. I miss you so much."

Brad was hurt. He kissed Michelle on the forehead and got up to leave. He stopped in the doorway and stared at his wife as she dozed off to sleep, holding the locket in her hand. He then retired to his bedroom.

Brad didn't believe in God or miracles. He simply hoped that if he talked loud enough and if there *was* a powerful existence of some kind, that someone, something—that higher being—would hear him say these words and give him guidance. "I don't know how much more of this I can take. I married for better or worse. I have been patient through the worst, so when will it get better?" He cut off the lights, turned over, and fell asleep.

* * *

Kathy didn't want to interrupt Michelle and Brad's marriage anymore. It was already rocky. If Michelle found out that Brad had been helping her financially, it could send her over the edge and be the end of their marriage. Kathy didn't want to be responsible for that. She decided to stop reaching out to Michelle and asking Brad for help.

She decided to take Michelle's advice and make amends with Jackie. Kathy did miss Jackie a lot. She built up the nerve and went to Jackie's house. She rung the doorbell and waited nervously. While she waited for someone to come to the door, she practiced her apology speech. Countless thoughts and what-ifs ran through her head. *What if she slams the door in my face? What if she cusses me out? What if Gerald comes to the door? What if she also had Gerald's baby? What if she doesn't want to ever see me again?*

Just when the what-ifs had scared Kathy enough to leave, Jackie opened the door. She was more than excited to see Kathy. She greeted her old friend as if nothing had ever happened between them.

Jackie picked up Kathy's daughter. "Oh my God," she gushed. "Come in. Come on in. It's so good to see you. Oh, look how cute this child is."

Tears swelled in Kathy's eyes as guilt settled in. "Jackie, I want to apol …"

Jackie interrupted, "No, don't. You don't need to."

"I do," Kathy insisted. "I want to apologize. You have been a very, very good friend—a best friend at that. I miss that, and I miss you. I lost a lot when I lost you. Please forgive me."

"You know what?" Jackie said. "I had forgiven you the same day I found out about your pregnancy. I was only mad at you for a minute. I was more upset at myself for letting a man come between us. I should have known better. He wasn't gonna treat me any different than he treated his wife or you."

"I was jealous because he had more feelings for you," Kathy admitted.

"Come on in the kitchen so I can get us something to eat," Jackie said. "We have a lot of catching up to do."

"This is a big house," Kathy said, as they went in.

Jackie showed Kathy around. "Do you get support from Gerald?" she asked.

"No, he doesn't claim her, and he doesn't want to see her."

"He's crazy."

"I bet he's still cheating on his wife," Kathy said.

"I guess you haven't heard."

"What? I haven't heard anything. What happened?"

"He caught his wife in their bed with another man—some man from her church. He shot them both. His wife's lover died, and she's paralyzed from the waist down. That little boy he highly praised, her last baby, isn't his."

"Wow, this is hard to believe. We all wanted to be his wife."

"Speak for yourself," Jackie said. "I didn't want him for a husband."

"Is he serving time?"

Jackie shook her head. "His lawyer and wife pleaded with the courts. His wife needed him to help with the kids and her. His business went down. Radio Burger doesn't get nearly half the business it used too."

"Now I know why his wife never got mad at him for being out all night. She took that time to cheat herself."

"What a hot mess. I feel sorry for her. She's stuck with him now." Jackie put a kettle on the stove to boil and pulled two cups from her cupboard.

"You know he has at least eight kids by different women. I don't know why I was so stupid over him."

"Stop beating yourself up. Something good did come out of all of this. You have this beautiful little girl."

"You're right. At least I still have one daughter who loves me."

"Oh yeah, how are Michelle and her husband?"

"I wouldn't know." Kathy's voice dropped and she looked out the window. "She still hates me. She refuses to talk to me. I was not invited to her wedding. Tony thought it would be in Michelle's best interest that I didn't come. My appearance would only upset her.

"You know over the years, Tony has become one arrogant ass bastard. If Michelle only knew the truth. He made me take Michelle to get that abortion. I begged him to let Michelle keep her baby. He wouldn't hear of it. He let me take all of the blame ."

The tea kettle sung, and Jackie turned the stove off. "I hope you don't tell her. You will be stirring up trouble, and it could backfire on you."

"No, I'm not going to tell her. What good would it do now anyway? She would only think I was trying to be manipulative again." She accepted the tea cup Jackie offered her. "Besides, I give up. I'm tired of being screamed at and cussed at. You should hear some of the things she says to me. I don't even know her anymore. I'm tired of being hurt and insulted by her. I still love her, but I'm done." She wiped away tears and spooned in sugar from the bowl Jackie had set down on the table. "I heard you were at the wedding."

Jackie blew into her tea cup and watched the steam rise from the hot liquid. "Randy and I were there, and I saw Donnie and his wife also. Michelle grew up to be a beautiful, sophisticated young woman. She looks like a model. And her husband's not so bad looking either ."

"Michelle's husband is very sweet. I really do like him. He wanted me at that wedding. He was going to fly us in. Tony found out and told me that if I showed up, he would have security escort me out."

"I asked him why you weren't there, and he told me you didn't want to come."

Kathy shook her head bitterly. "Tony and his wife think they are royalty, like they are better than people."

"I know," Jackie agreed. "He didn't say too much to me. I felt out of place."

Kathy sipped her tea. "No one poor was on the guest list."

"So that explains why I didn't feel comfortable. I was the poorest person there." Jackie laughed. "The wedding was beautiful, and Michelle was breathtaking. She was excited to have me there."

"I saw the wedding on disk. Brad mailed it to me. If Michelle has her way I probably won't ever get to see any of my grandchildren."

"She'll come around one day," Jackie said soothingly. "It's gonna take something to happen to bring you two back together again. You will get a second chance. I know it."

Kathy shook her head. "Are you psychic or something? How can you predict that? It's been years, and she hasn't come around yet. It seems like she hates me more and more every day."

"I just know. Trust me. She will be your daughter again."

* * *

Soon Kathy was going to Jackie house every day. They would drink coffee and talk like old times. Kathy found a job, and Jackie babysat for free. Jackie enjoyed having a child around the house again. She only saw her grandkids during Christmastime. She cooked every day, so Kathy and her child could have a home-cooked meal. Jackie gave Kathy a spare key to let herself in. Some mornings, Kathy came over too early and Jackie wouldn't be out of bed.

One afternoon over coffee and bagels, Kathy and Jackie started reminiscing about the good old days. "I miss all the kids who grew up in the Hamptons," Jackie said.

"I'd like to know what some of them are doing today."Reply Kathy

"You remember how we used to play games with them and throw cookout parties for them."

"Not me," Kathy said. "You did all the hands-on stuff. I sat around and watched. Those kids looked up to you Jackie."

Jackie smiled. "I tried to be the parent they didn't have. I've read about some of them in the papers and on the news channel. Donnie and his wife are both lawyers, and he is governor of Washington. His Granddad died from cancer. He left Donnie a substantial amount of money. I heard he's a billionaire. His granddad was funny. Remember the stuff Donnie would tell us about his grandfather? You couldn't hate the old man. It would be so funny. I liked him.

"Sean is a manager of a grocery store. Chris and Foster are rap singers. They're called the C-F Mooves. Michael opened up a soul food restaurant. He is now a she. He had a sex change operation. Her new name is Me'chele. The food is good."

"It ought to be," Kathy said with a grin. "You taught him—or her—how to cook."

"I can't remember the girls' names. They hung around Hallie. One is a porn star, one is a model. That Tiffany girl is a nurse. Liz is secretary for a law firm. Marge owns a cleaning company. And then there's your daughter, the scientist slash doctor and author."

"And don't forget your sons," Kathy chimed in. "They got out of the projects, and they're doing well too."

"I'm proud of them too. I just wish I could see Jamal and my grandkids more." She brightened up. "Let me show you some pictures of my grandkids." Jackie pulled out her photo albums to show Kathy, explaining each picture.

"Baker Street is not the same anymore," Kathy said with a sigh.

"I know. It was changing before I left."

Snake, Lee, Bighead, Charles, and James hadn't yet corrupted the neighborhood while Jackie was there. Now they were way out of control. Anyone who knew them was afraid of them. Snake was the biggest, most dangerous drug dealer and gangster around. He had a bad reputation.

"I wish I could have been more like you. All the kids that knew you speak highly of you and still respect you today." Getting to her feet, she put her plate in the sink. "Well I need to be going. I'll be here early in the morning so we can drink some coffee together."

"Use your key, just in case I don't hear the doorbell."

"Okay, I will," Kathy agreed. "See ya tomorrow. Love you."

They kissed each other on each cheek. Jackie stood in the doorway until Kathy drove out of sight.

Early the next morning, Kathy arrived at Jackie's house to drop the baby off and have coffee with her. She rang the doorbell couple of times before she let herself in. She called out to Jackie to let her know she was there. She laid her daughter, who was still asleep, down in the room that Jackie had fixed up just for her. She called out to Jackie again. "We're here. I'll get the coffee started."

Jackie still didn't answer.

After Kathy had fixed a pot of coffee, she drank a cup and read part of the newspaper. Jackie should have been up by now,she whisper.. She decided to go and wake Jackie up. It was getting close to the time for Kathy to leave for work. In her room, Jackie lay there, not responding to her calls.

"Jackie, get your butt up, girl. I have to leave." Kathy walked closer and kept calling Jackie. When she touched Jackie, her friend didn't move. "Oh God, Jackie!" Kathy screamed, realization dawning on her. "Wake up, please wake up! Don't you do this now. Wake up."

She wept and nervously dail 9-1-1. "I need help!" she screamed. "My friend is not responding. She's unconscious. Please send help now."

The operator asked a lot of questions, and Kathy tried to answer them as best she could. She gave Jackie's address.

In minutes, an EMS team had arrived. They rushed Jackie to Memorial Hospital.

A series of tests showed Jackie had had a massive stroke and was brain dead. She was on life support. The doctor asked Kathy if she was family and told her to contact Jackie's sons.

Kathy contacted Jamal. Jamal called Travis. Kathy called Brad, who told Michelle who called Donnie. Word spread quickly about Jackie's condition. Everyone who knew Jackie called, sent flowers and cards, or came to visit. Michelle and her husband flew in. Jamal and his wife and Travis and Randy were all in the room with Jackie.

Kathy never left Jackie's side.

The doctors told Jamal and Travis that it was time for them to consider taking Jackie off life support. She had suffered severe brain damage, and it wasn't reversible. Days went by. Finally, Jamal, as the oldest, decided to take his mother off life support. Travis was against doing so. Travis and

Jamal argued continually. There was times when hospital security had to be called in.

"You got to understand," Jamal said to his brother "Mama wouldn't want to live like this."

"Who made you God?" Travis demanded. "This will be murder."

"It's not murder. She's brain dead. Look at her," Jamal said, pointing at Jackie lying in her hospital bed, "just look at her will ya. She's not here anymore."

"Shut up," Travis said. "You don't know what you're talking about. You never care for Mom. Ever since you and Hallie broke up, you haven't treated Mom the same. I've heard of people coming out of their comas."

"The doctors said there's not a chance Mom's coming out of this coma. I do love my mom. You can't say that I don't love her. This isn't easy for me either you know."

"This isn't easy for you, you say," Travis shot back. "I'm the one who calls her every day. I'm the one who visits her every chance I get. You didn't. You called or visited Mom once a year. You got your family. You don't need Mom anymore. She's all the family I got."

"You got me," Jamal said. "I'm family. I love you, and I love Mom enough not to let her suffer like this. Her doctor said she will be in a vegetative state for the rest of her life."

"Doctors are not God," Travis protested. "And you aren't either."

"I'm sorry, Travis, that you feel this way. I love Mom too much to let her live like this. I told her doctor to go ahead. In the morning at 8:00 a.m. is when they will shut off the life support. We have time to say our last good-byes. I'm sorry, man."Jackie assign Jamal power of attorney.She knew Travis wouldn't take her off life support if something were to happen to her.. "If you go through with this, it will be the end of us," Travis said, his face flooding with anger. "I will never, as long as I breathe, claim you as my brother."

"You can't mean that," Jamal said gently. "Mama would want us to always stay close. We are all we got. We are brothers."

Travis turned away. "No brother of mine would do this," he said through gritted teeth. "This is wrong, and you know it. I don't even know you anymore. I'm not going to be here for this. I hope you rot in hell. All of you!"

Travis kissed and said his good-bye to his mother. "Mama, I love you so much. I don't want you to leave me. I thought mothers lived forever. They're taking you away from me. I'm going to miss you so much. I don't want you to leave me. You're the best mother in the world. Prove them wrong and wake up out of this coma. Please come back. Wake up, Mama, wake up. I'm going to miss you so much." With that, he broke into sobs, gathering his unconscious mother into his arms. After saying his goodbyes Travis stormed past Jamal without uttering a word to his brother and went straight to the airport, where he caught the first flight out. No one would ever hear from Travis again.

The next day, Jamal and his family, along with Kathy, Randy, Michelle, and Brad, were in the hospital room with Jackie when the life support was turned off. Many people stopped by to say good-bye. Jamal looked around for his brother, but understood why he didn't show. He knew Travis would be at the funeral and he hoped they could mend their differences.

Michelle cut her eyes in Kathy's direction so she could get a good look at her child.

"Michelle, this is a good time to make things right with your mother," Brad whisper in Michelle's ear. "Look at her. She's all alone. She just lost her best friend."

"She's got her daughter," Michelle said. "She's not alone."

"This could be your mother lying there," Brad said gently. "This is the right time to make up. At least meet your sister."

"Look, let's not discuss this," Michelle replied. "It's not the right time."

"When is the right time, Michelle? To you, there's never a right time."

"Look," she said, "I'm trying. I'm seeing a counselor. She said I would know when I'm ready. You were there when she said that."

"Yeah," Brad replied, "I was there. You don't want to let go of Ron. You're not even trying to make our marriage work. I have been patient, but now my patience is wearing out. I can't keep living like this. I want a wife. I can't complete with a ghost. I won't win. If you want this marriage to work, you've got to let go of the past and start working on the future. I won't live like this anymore. I do love you. I really do. But it's time to make some changes.

"I will be staying at your mother's apartment. If you want to talk, you can reach me there. I'm giving you a choice. It's me or your ghost. If you haven't come to a decision after the funeral, I will be moving out and flying to Mexico for an immediate divorce."

Michelle held her locket tightly as Brad spoke. It was obvious to Brad who Michelle had chosen.

Kathy was too distraught to deal with Michelle's rejection. Kathy couldn't handle losing the only friend she'd ever had. She was standing in a corner by herself when Brad went over to console her. Tears flooded from her eyes as she watched her only dear friend slip away into another life. She couldn't bring herself to say good-by. Kathy fainted once the doctor announced the time of death, and Brad was there to catch her fall.

Michelle kissed Jackie on the forehead. She then left and went back to her hotel room without saying a word to Brad.

Everyone started to disband slowly. Only Jamal and Randy were left in the room. Randy rushed out of the hospital room. He sat inside his car and kept hitting the dashboard. "Why do you keep taking the people I love away from me," he said, directing his question at God. "My sister, my brother, and now Ms. Jackie—what have I done to deserve so much pain? Why do you keep taking away people I love?"Tell me what am I being punish for! TELL ME,I DEMAND TO KNOW! Tell me whyyyyy,. Randy cried out.

Randy laid his head on the car dash and wept. "Why?" he repeated over and over. "God, why?"

Jamal stayed with his mother until the hospital staff carried her away. Jamal hugged her and kissed her on the lips. "Rest, mother," he said softly. "Your work here is done. God needs you to help care for the children in heaven. I'll see you there one day. I love you, Mom. I miss you already." He cried silently.

Jamal and his wife made funeral preparations. They couldn't reach Travis for his input. The funeral was held at a convention center. So many people came. Jackie had touched so many lives. People lined up outside waiting to get in just to view the body.

Michelle and Brad remained distant. They hadn't spoken since he'd given her the ultimatum.

Only a handful of people were aloud on the burial grounds. Each one approached the casket. Gerald showed up with a dozen roses. When he approached the casket, he places the flowers and kissed Jackie on the lips. "I should have married you," he whispered. "I wouldn't be in this mess I'm in. You're all I think about. We had some good times together."

When Michelle approached the open casket, she took the locket from around her neck and placed it in Jackie's hand. Michelle bent over to Jackie and whispered, "Take good care of him for me, and tell him I'm not abandoning him. I will carry him in my heart forever. I know he is in good company with you. Good-bye my love."

Brad and Kathy watched as Michelle place the locket inside the casket. She turned and walked toward her husband and hugged her mother and said, "I'm so sorry."

They both cried as they embraced each other. They watched as the casket was lowered into the ground. Michelle knew that Ron was safe in Jackie's care. After the funeral, Brad saw a different Michelle. She was a woman who was ready to be his wife.

Some of Jamal and Jackie's closest friends gathered at Jackie's home. They laughed, cried, ate, and shared memories of the past. They introduced each other to their families and caught up on the present. They all credited Jackie for their successes.

Michelle was an affectionate person and wasn't shy about showing it in public. She would always walk up to her husband and kissed him passionately on his lips. She holds his hands, rub her nose against his nose or playfully hit his but in public. This was the Michelle Brad had longed for.

Everyone agreed the service was nice and Jackie looked beautiful. She looked like her younger self. Some of the guests started asking where Travis was. They hadn't seen him at the funeral or at the burial site.

Michelle and Brad approached Donnie and his wife. "I tried to pay for Jackie's hospital bill," Michelle said. "The billing clerk said it was all taken care of. I want to take care of all Jackie's hospital and funeral expenses. What was the cost so I can write you a check?"

"Oh, no," Donnie began.

"Well let me pay half or pay for one or the other. I insist. Jackie's been a dear to me. I want to do my part."

"No that's not what I meant," Donnie explained. "I didn't pay it. I tried to and was told the same thing. If you and I didn't pay the bills, then I assume Randy did. After all, he brought her this house. I'm giving Randy a check for the cost of the bills."

"Don't write the check just yet. I want to share the cost too. Let's get Randy over here."Reply Michelle"Here he comes now," Kathy said.

Randy was walking toward them. "How you holding up?" Donnie asked.

"I feel all alone now," Randy answered. "My brother, now Jackie. But I don't want to get into that right now. Look, I don't know which one of you paid Jackie's medical and funeral expenses, but I want to.

"We thought you had paid them," Michelle interrupted.

"If we didn't pay the bills, then who did?"

Michelle and Randy looked puzzled.

"We're the only ones who can afford to pay the expenses. The billing clerks at the hospital and the funeral home said everything was paid in full with cash. They couldn't disclose to me who paid, as the payer wanted to remain anonymous." answer Randy

Jamal was making his way around the room, thanking everyone for coming. He made a speech to his closest friends, believing Michelle, Donnie, and Randy were responsible for paying all his mother's bills. He ended his speech by saying, "I want to thank you all for taking care of my mother's needs and lifting the burden from my brother and me. I can't thank you enough. This is what true friendship is about. I love you guys"

No one told Jamal anything different. Donnie, Michelle, and Randy all felt someone among them had paid Jackie's medical and funeral expenses but didn't want the others to know. That person didn't want to share the cost. Paying Jackie's bills was the ultimate way to give back. Jackie had given so much too so many.

As the day was coming to an end, no one wanted this to be their last good-bye. Randy promised to give everyone VIP Super Bowl tickets. Donnie promised to invite them to one of his cabins in the mountains for skiing, hiking, and ice fishing. Michelle promised to invite then to her masquerade party, a big socialite event that she hosted once a year. The invite list included A-list celebrities, some politicians, and the president of the United States. The rich and the famous would be there.

*   *   *

The promises the trio made were never kept. They were too busy with their families and their careers. Their paths would never cross again.

Donnie paid for Geraldine's nursing home expenses but never visited. Jamal continued to search for his brother. He hired a private investigator. No trace of Travis was found. It was like he had vanished from the face of the earth. Jamal would never know whether his brother was dead or alive. He never gave up on the search

*   *   *

Since letting go of the past, Michelle made love to her husband in a whole different way. He couldn't believe how good she was in bed. Brad fell in love with Michelle all over again. She wasn't cold-hearted anymore; she was more sensitive.

She agreed with her husband that her mother and sister could come live with them. Michelle told Brad she was ready to have his baby.

Kathy was tremendously excited to have her daughter back and to be getting out of the projects. She tried to catch up on all that she missed throughout Michelle's life. She could hardly catch her breath.

Brad told Kathy to only pack what she needed. She shouldn't bring furniture or appliance. Once they arrived in California, he and Michelle would buy whatever she and the little one needed.

Kathy packed photos, toys, and clothes. She had longed for this day. She could hardly wait to get to California and start their new life together. But first, Michelle wanted to take a last walk through the neighborhood. Kathy tried to talk her out of it. "Michelle, this is not a safe neighborhood anymore to be walking around. Someone's always getting shot or robbed."

"Mom, I'll be okay. I just want to see what happened to the ones who didn't make it out and see what I can do to help them."

Michelle headed out the door, not afraid of what could happen.

Kathy wasn't going to let any harm come to her daughter, even if it meant losing her own life protecting her. She had just gotten her daughter back. She wasn't about to lose her now. "I'm going with you," she said.

"You don't have to," Michelle replied. "I'll be all right."

"I want to. Besides, I haven't walked through the hood in years."

They left Brad to babysit and pack. Michelle and Kathy talked while walking. "You're right," Michelle said. "It's not the same neighborhood. I wonder if it ever will be."

"I don't believe so," Kathy replied. "These kids today are so bad. They don't want you telling them what to do."

"Not all kids are bad. When a few neighborhood kids get in trouble, people assume all the kids are trouble. We need someone like Jackie again. She was a godsend. Mom, why you weren't more like Jackie?"

"I don't know," Kathy replied. "She told me she wasn't happy in that new neighborhood. It was too quiet. No kids were around. She came alive when I brought your sister over."

"That's what kept her alive. I read Jackie's medical records. She was really sick, Mom. Her depression made it worse. I'm surprised she lived this long. Jackie was at her happiest when she was around children. I'm going to open up a youth center in her name here."

Kathy smiled. "That's a good idea. I know if she was alive she would love that. Jackie had brought so many people together. It's heartbreaking to know that Travis isn't speaking to his brother. They were once so close. It's hard to believe that Jackie's death would break her own family apart."

"The death of a loved one isn't easy on your heart," Michelle replied softly. "Some people would rather have their hearts ripped out than to feel the loss of that loved one. If they don't seek help, the loss could have an everlasting emotional effect that could end in tragedy. I hope both Jamal and Travis seek professional help."

Kathy rubbed Michelle's back gently as she spoke. "Do you think Travis will ever forgive Jamal?"

"I hope so. I surely hope so, for Jackie's sake.Michelle change the subject. Let's go to the corner park."

"I wish you wouldn't," Kathy replied. "There's so much drugs and violence at the corner park. The gangs and dealers have taken over the park."

"Mom, you can go back. I'm going on. I want to see if I run into anyone I know."

"It's a dangerous place," Kathy warned. People have gotten killed and rape there."

"If your reason for leaving the Hamptons is fear of getting killed," Michelle replied. "You do know you have a chance of being murdered anywhere. There's no such thing as a crime-free neighborhood anywhere."As they approach the park,

Young boys yelled sexual overtures at them. Drug dealers, thinking the women were there to buy, ran up to show off their drugs. Kathy and Michelle continued walking, ignoring both. Kathy pulled on Michelle's arm to get her to walk faster. Sounds filled the air—sirens, music, crying children, and everyone talking at once.

Michelle approached a drunken man who looked familiar to her and asked. "Hi. How are you doing? My name is Michelle. I'm looking for Lee-Lee Garrison. Do you know him?"

"Give me some money," the drunken man responded.

"Where can I locate Lee?"

"What business you have?" the drunken man replied. "Are you a cop or something?"

"We're friends," Kathy interrupted, "and his street name is Smokie."

"Oh Shit," the drunken man replied. "He's around the corner at Taylor's Funeral home. Hey, let me have five dollars for food."

Michelle reaches in her jean pants pocket and gave him a hundred dollar bill.

Kathy pulled on Michelle so they could get away quickly.

"It's good to know he's working," Michelle said. "Let's go see him."

"Michelle, it's getting late," Kathy said. "We shouldn't be walking through the neighborhood after dark."

"It will be ok. I'll call Brad to pick us up or we can take a cab. I want to see if Lee needs anything or if I can make a difference in his life."

"I wish I could have done more in this neighborhood," Kathy lamented.

Once they arrived at Taylor's Funeral Home, Michelle asked the director if she could see Mr. Lee Garrison. Without Michelle or Kathy realizing what was about to happen, the director took them to a room where Lee's body lay. The women were shocked.

"I thought he was working here," Michelle said. "I didn't know he was …. What happened? I saw him at the hospital and at Jackie's funeral. How did this happen? I mean, what happened?"

"He was gunned down," the funeral director told them. "They tortured him badly, poor soul. It took a lot of work to get his face to look human again.This is what can happen when you dealing with the wrong crowd."

Michelle was sobbing.

"He did look nervous at Jackie's funeral," Kathy recalled.

"I wish I had talked to him," said Michelle. "Maybe I could have helped in some way. This shouldn't have happened."

Michelle told the funeral director she would be responsible for all Lee's funeral expenses and that she'd pick out a better casket than the one he was in. She wrote out a check for the cost.

"Lee's death doesn't surprise me," Kathy told her. "He was hanging with Snake. Everyone who knows Snake knows he is the biggest drug dealer in town, and no one crosses him."

"Let's go," Michelle said. "I'm tired. There's too much sadness here. Let's go home to California. There's nothing here anymore."

Brad had finished with the last of the packing and had loaded the rental car. When Michelle and Kathy arrived back on Baker Street, they saw Donnie's grandmother leaving Victoria's apartment.

"That was Donnie's grandmother," Kathy said. "I would like to know what that was all about."

"Are we ready to go?" Brad asked.

Michelle and Kathy both said yes.

"Well let's go. Our flight leaves in two hours. We need to leave now so we can check our luggage in."

Kathy and her daughter sat in the backseat. Brad drove, and Michelle sat in the passenger seat. They pulled out of the driveway slowly, being careful of the small kids playing in the street. The sun was beginning to set. The sky was filled with many different colors, it has never looked more beautiful.

"Mama, where are we going?" Kathy's youngest daughter asked.

"Home," Kathy replied, "We're going home, baby."

The child pointed at their apartment and said, "I thought that was our home."

"We are going to our new home," Kathy replied. "We're going to love it there."

Kathy turned to look the neighborhood over for the last time. She blinked twice to clear her focus. She saw a vision of Jackie sitting on the porch smiling and waving good-bye. Tears swelled in Kathy's eyes as she waved back.

"Mama, who are you waving at?" the child asked.

"Oh," she said softly, "I'm waving to a very good, good friend."

Michelle heard the emotion in Kathy's voice.

Michelle asked the child to sit up front with her.

"We have the same name," the little girl said.

"Our names are similar but not the same," Michelle explained. "I'm Michelle with an *M*, and you're Nichelle with an *N*."

"Why did my mama gave us similar names?" Nichelle asked.

"Because your mama is my mama. You're my little sister. We are going to have so much fun together."Michelle gave Nichelle a long hug.

Kathy kept staring at Jackie's old apartment until she couldn't see it anymore. "Thank you," she whispered. She blew a kiss in the direction of Jackie's apartment. She wiped her eyes to keep the tears from running down her face.

* * *

At the pool room where Snake and his gang hung out, one of his gang members approached him and said, "We traced everywhere. His girlfriend, his family—no one was seen with anything new and none of them know anything. No one has seen him spending a large sum of money."

"Keep searching," Snake yelled. "That kind of money doesn't just disappear." Snake was so angry he broke his cue stick in half.

"He was seen at the hospital," another gang member offered, "and at some old bat funeral."

Snake interrupted him in a rage. "Ms. Jackie, do you hear me! It's Ms. Jackie to you. I better not ever hear anyone disrespecting her. That goes for everyone and anyone. I will put a bullet between your eyes and the eyes of all your family, so help me." He yelled the threat so that everyone in the pool room could hear him.

"I'm sorry, man," the gangster replied. "I didn't mean to disrespect Ms. Jackie,"

Snake motioned to a third gang member. He whisper in his ear. "Get back with me ASAP and keep this between us," Few days passed.

When the gangster got Snake the information he was looking for, Snake was shaken up. He ordered everyone out of the pool room. He got sick to his stomach and vomited. Tears filled his eyes as he screamed out, "What have I done? Damn you, Lee. Why didn't you tell me? She was like a mother to me too. You should have told me. We were all like Jackie's children, man. None of this should have happened." Snake sat in the pool room alone repeating, "You should have told me" over and over. You should have told me.

* * *

Since Jackie's death, Randy put all his energy into his games. He was more focused. He became faster and better. He became an all-star player. He was known as the best wide receiver in history. He was doing commercials, TV sitcoms, and movie appearances. He had tennis shoes designed in his name.

He ran a football training camp for underprivileged kids in his brother's name and donated money to his former high school for a new football stadium and uniforms. The school named the new stadium "Ron's Stadium and hung a large picture of Ron and Randy in the entrance area. Once a year, Randy would go to high schools to talk to the teens about how drugs and unprotect sex could ruin your life.

* * *

Vera never liked football. Nor did she keep up with the players. She lived in South Carolina with her husband, where no one knew she had sons.

One day, she was home sick from her job as a housekeeper at a local hotel. She saw a commercial with her son in it, Randy, mentioning the tennis shoes named after him. Vera's face lit up.

She Google Randy. What she found excited her. Randy was worth eighty million dollars. She started screaming with excitement. "I'm rich! I'm rich!" Jumping up and down, she babbled an explanation to her husband, Leroy.

"Stop acting stupid," Leroy replied. "You don't have a son."

Lisa was, by then, sixteen. She was overweight and lazy. She talked back, ate a lot, and refused to clean up after herself. Vera was scared of Lisa. Lisa had knocked her down once and threatened to kill her and her husband. Leroy didn't try to discipline Lisa. He would tell Vera to handle her own daughter. Vera tried telling Lisa to clean her room, wash the dishes, go to school, pick up after herself, and turn her music down. Lisa never did anything Vera asked her to do.

Lisa saw her brother, Randy, on television. Seeing him gave her hope that, one day soon, she and her brother would be together again.

Lisa had heard about Ron's death through Jackie. She had begged Vera to let her go to the funeral, but Vera had refused. After that day, Lisa had decided to make Vera's life miserable. She'd lost all respect for her mother.

Soon Vera was bragging to her coworkers, her neighbors, and friends that she had a famous, rich son. No one believed her. She'd never mentioned that she had boys before. People she boasted to asked why she was living in that small house and working just as hard as they were. People start laughing at her and calling her a pathological liar.

Lisa wouldn't get involved. When Vera asked her to tell someone about her brother, she would go to her room and slam her bedroom door.

"Just wait. I'll show all of y'all when I get my money," Vera told Leroy. "I'm coming back riding in a limousine and wearing diamonds and a fur coat. I'm going to Paris and all over the world. I need to start packing."

"Packing for what?" Leroy smirked. "You ain't going nowhere. That boy is not your son."

"Like hell," Vera snapped. "I'm sick of this dump. You ain't shit, and you don't have shit. You got me down here living like a slave in this small, one-bathroom, old, ragged house."

"At least it's paid for and I got a roof over my head," Leroy shot back.

Vera yelled excitedly to Lisa, "Pack your clothes. We getting the hell out of this old dump. We got to leave soon before those money hungry whores try to get their hands on my son's money."

Lisa put her headphones on to drown out Vera's voice.

"I have an idea," Vera told Leroy. Let Lisa stay here and I will send for her after I get settled."

"Hell no," he replied. "You must be out of your mind. Now I know you're crazy. You are not dumping her on me. Take her with you. She's hardheaded and lazy. She is nothing but trouble."

Lisa had once told Leroy that if he thought he was going to discipline her, he should think again. She would lie and tell the police he was sexually assaulting her. He had been scare of her ever since. He made sure he was never alone with her. If he came home and Vera wasn't there, he would sit in the car or go to a nearby restaurant. He surely wasn't going to let her stay.

"You're a coward," Vera taunted. "You're scared of a sixteen-year-old girl. She tells you to jump, you jump. Some kind of man you are."

"You ain't no different. You want to drop your problem on me. You and I both know that, once you leave this girl here, you ain't gonna send for her. So if you do leave, take her with you. If she wasn't so bad and hardheaded, I would say yes. And for the record, once you leave you can't come back."

"What the hell would I want to come back to this for," Vera said cruelly. "I will never set foot in this old shack again."

"Good. Get your shit and go and don't forget your daughter. I can finally get some peace and quiet now. Plus I can keep my ragged old shack clean again," Leroy replied sarcastically. "Don't forget to leave my door keys."

Vera and Lisa pack all they owned in the truck and backseat of Vera's car and headed out. She tried to get a phone number for Randy but couldn't.

Lisa didn't know what kind of reception they were going to receive from Randy. It had been years since they'd seen each other. Once they arrived at Randy's place, if he didn't accept them, Lisa planned to never return with Vera, even if that meant living on the streets.

Getting to their destination took a long time because the car broke down twice. Vera didn't know how to get in touch with Randy, so she contacted a trashy gossip magazine. The magazine staff was glad to pay Vera, just to get some dirt on Randy. He was too squeaky clean.

Randy was always traveling, so it was hard to connect with him. When word got around that Randy's mother was in town, he didn't jump with excitement. He just went on with his everyday life like she didn't exist. He told a reporter his mother was dead.

Vera continued trying to see Randy. When she realized he wasn't interest in seeing her, she decided she would blackmail him. She hadn't come this far to get humiliated by not getting her share of the money.

Randy had taken a role in a sitcom, and he was on location shooting for one of the episodes when the trashy gossip magazine decided to arrange for a reunion. Randy had no idea of what was about to happen. The magazine staff knew this would be a top-selling article. A few questions had to be answered, including why Randy had said his mother was dead if Vera was, in fact, his mother and, if she was, why he refused to acknowledge her.

The reporters hung around like vultures. TV cameras were everywhere when Vera interrupted his shot. Randy was furious. He knew Vera was using him. She made sure all the cameras were there to film their reunion, knowing he wouldn't reject her with TV cameras around. Vera ran to Randy, as if it was a happy homecoming for them both. He pushed her away and walked off the set. She ran behind him to keep up appearances.

A reporter put the mic in Vera's face. "Why wasn't Randy thrilled about this reunion?" she asked.

Another reporter chimed in. "What happened to cause him to pull away from you and storm out like that?

"There are rumors that you are not his mother but some greedy, money-hungry blackmailer," a third reporter noted.

Vera was embarrassed as the questions came at her from all directions. She knew her friends, coworkers, and husband could be watching this on TV. She pushed past the reporters to find Randy. Vera was vindictive. Randy had embarrassed her on national television, and she was determined to make him look just as bad.

Lisa was standing in the shadows. She didn't want any part of Vera's circus. She didn't want Randy to think she was after his money also.

The reporter who had first asked Vera about the reunion's failure followed Randy for days without him knowing. Randy went to Ron's memorial sight. It was a marker Randy had built since there had been no body to bury. Randy buried some of Ron' favorite items—things they'd shared growing up together. This was a place where he could connect with Ron. He would come here to talk to Ron, leaving flowers with a football attached to the bunch.

Vera was talking to reporters. She told her version of why Randy had refused to see her to trashy gossip magazine. The story she was telling could ruin Randy's reputation and cause him to lose his endorsements. Vera didn't care. If he wouldn't share with her his success and wealth, she wanted to destroy him instead.

While Vera was talking to the reporter, the reporter who had followed Randy found Lisa and asked her version of the truth. What Lisa told the reporter and her cameraman brought tears to both of their eyes. Lisa told them how Vera would leave them for months without food all by themselves, how she would beat and call her brothers derogatory names, especially Ron. She'd been the hardest on him, calling him stupid and ugly and telling him he'd never amount to anything. She would hit him with anything she got her hands on. When he'd died, she hadn't gone to her own son's funeral.

When Lisa finished, the mood changed. No one felt sorry for Vera anymore. The reporter called her colleague who was interviewing Vera. Then she called her editors. "Have I got a cover story," she announced. "Randy's sister just told me a story that is heartbreaking and unbelievable. Did you know Randy had a brother who was just as good at football as him? The brother would have been the star in this family, but he died. Get this—his own mother refused to go to her son's funeral. She abandoned them when they were children to be with some man she met online."

The reporter who had been interviewing Vera earlier later confirmed his colleague's story. "It's true," she told their editors. "I did some research on this woman. I asked her if she wanted to visit her son's memorial, said I'd take her. She told me no. When I asked if she knew what was on the marker, she switched the subject. I get the feeling that this woman is here for money. I told her anyway what the marker read—here lies the world's greatest brother."

"Then it's true," said the reporter who'd interviewed Lisa, as she entered the office. "This woman came here for money. She still doesn't give a damn about her kids. I have an idea. Let's write Randy's biography. We need to get the truth out before Vera ruins him. I know this will be a best seller. I can feel it. We can donate all the money to a fund that helps abandoned children."

"How can we get it done so quickly?" her colleague asked.

"We have to do lots of research, and we can get other reporters to help," she replied. "I can fly to North Carolina and interview people who knew the family, and then I'll interview Vera's husband in South Carolina. You can interview Randy's friends and the players on his team that knew him."

"No one knew he went through hell like this," her fellow reporter commented. "He put on a brave face."

"Yeah, the mom sounds like a real bitch from hell. She came here to destroy her son. You should have heard what she said, knowing it could ruin him. I want to make sure she crawls back up under the rock she crawled out from. Randy doesn't need any more pain in his life. Are we all on board?" She faced a group of cameramen and reporters who'd gathered to hear the story.

They all agreed to help protect Randy from his greedy, dirty, low-life, so-called mother.

The two reporters who'd originally interviewed Randy's mom and sister set up a reunion between Lisa and Randy. Being reunited with his sister was the happiest moment of Randy's life.

Lisa was happy but sad because she couldn't share this moment with Ron. Tears flowed down her cheeks as she thought of all the time she missed. They went to Ron's memorial sight. "Forgive me for not being here for you," Lisa said through her tears. "I'm so sorry for what you went through. I am never going to forget you. I miss you so much. I wish you were here.."

Randy put his arms around his sister, who'd broken down into sobs. "Now that you're here, everything's going to be all right. We can be a family again. No one's going to pull us apart again."

Randy petitioned the court and received guardianship of Lisa. He put her in a private school, where she excelled. Vera was glad to get rid of Lisa.

The book, *Abandoned*, was released. It didn't take long for it to be on the *New York Times* Best Sellers' list. The book was made into a movie. Its popularity also revived people's interest in Michelle's *Till Death Do Us Part*, which once again graced the Best sellers' list.

Some of the people who saw the movie or read the book *Abandoned* called Vera names, such as slut, whore, no-good, dumbass, or bitch. She was in a restaurant one day and a table of customers heckled and threw food at her until she left. One man spit on her and said, "Even dogs take care of their pups." Every where she went someone would recognize her and ridicule her.

The reporter who'd interviewed Lisa paid Vera a visit. She gave Vera a copy of the book. "I thought you might want to read this before the movie version goes out in theaters everywhere," she said. "You've experienced dislike now. Wait until the movie is out. You will know what it's like to be on the other end of being abused. Tell me, how can you live with yourself? I can't believe you expected Randy to welcome you with open arms."

"I don't give a damn what you think about me," Vera spat. "Randy is my son. He's supposed to take care of me."

"Like you took care of your sons," the reporter shot back. "You are a joke."

"He can give me a million dollars, and I will go away. He'll never have to hear from me again. Don't I get something out of this book of lies you wrote about me?"

"Your share went to child abuse charities. I have good and bad news for you, honey. The good news is this—here's fifty thousand dollars."

Vera smiled and grabbed the check, already thinking of how she was going to spend her money.

"The bad news is that you get nothing else. So make it last."

The cameraman who'd accompanied the reporter on the visit addressed Vera "If you so much as try to blackmail Randy or contact him for any reason, I will kill you myself, you hear me." He turned to the reporter, as they walked back toward their car. "I wouldn't have given her shit. She's better off dead." He paused, noticing his colleague's distraught look. "Hey, are you all right. I've never seen you this upset before."

"Randy is a clean-cut, decent guy. He's a private person,he don't do drugs,he don't drink,he don't even smoke cigarettes.. I've seen kids with a mother like his and they turn out just like his brother did," the reporter replied. "Randy was the lucky one,he's a good person and I hope he stays that way."

"Women like Vera need to have their wombs ripped out while they are alert and feeling every agonizing moment."

"Be careful," the reporter said. "You're beginning to sound like a maniac."

*   *   *

Vera took the money and partied like a rock star, not realizing that fifty thousand dollars won't get you far. She was broke in six months. She was put out of the penthouse she'd been staying in, and the beamer she'd leased was repossessed. She was overdrawn on all her credit cards. Her bills were piling high. She needed more money but was afraid to ask. She tried to get a job, but no one would hire her.

Randy wouldn't give interviews or talk about the book abandoned. Lisa became overprotective of her brother. When she heard Vera was trying to contact him for money, Lisa made sure none of their mother's messages made it to Randy. Lisa hated Vera.

Vera was enduring a lot more backlash. The movie showed the cruel mistreatment Ron had suffered at his mother's hand. Vera was afraid for her life. She was getting death threats. People were calling her the same names she had once called Ron. She had things thrown at her just like she had thrown things at Ron.

Vera had no place to go. She decided to call her husband. "Leroy, it's me Vera," she said nervously. "I miss you so much. I want us to try to work things out. I'm coming home."

"Oh, no no," Leroy replied. "Not here. This is not your home anymore. Remember I told you that once you walked out this door, you couldn't come back."

"Please," Vera said. "I have no place to go. I want to come home. No one likes me here."

"Yeah, I know," Leroy replied. "I saw the movie *Abandoned*, and no one here likes you either. I'm sorry. I can't allow you back here. People will start hating me. You didn't have to lie about having those boys. I would have accepted them like they were my own. I always wanted kids. As bad as your daughter was, I treated her well. Your boys could have stayed here. I would have moved us into a bigger house. You lied. I didn't know I'd married a fucking monster."

"Please, I have no place to go," Vera begged. "That book was a lie. I don't have any money for food or a place to lay my head. It's getting cold. At least send me some money."

"You didn't care if your kids got food or a warm place to stay," Leroy replied. "What makes you deserving of any better treatment? You know all of this could have been avoided. If you hated your sons, instead of mistreating them, you should have put them up for adoption. You didn't go to your son's funeral. Hell no. I don't want you here. Remember what you said before you left. Who would want to live in a small, old, ragged shack?" He slammed the phone down.

I wish I had gotten to know those boys, Leroy thought.What a shame.

Vera was scared and all alone, it was getting dark. "What's gonna happen to me?" Vera said, talking to herself. "I'm cold and hungry. I've never been without a place to live. I don't know what to do. I don't want to live in a shelter with those kinds of people. Please, God, help me. It's wrong for my children to treat me like this. All that money Randy has. They're living in that mansion and wearing expensive clothes. It's not fair to be mistreated like this."

Vera wandered around in the streets. She'd sleep in a shelter until someone recognized her. Once, she was gang beaten badly. Her front teeth were knocked out. She lost the sight in one of her eyes. After that incident in the shelter, she made her home in alleys. She drank cheap wine when it was offered and begged for food and money. Vera was faced with learning how to survive on the streets. She did whatever it took to do so. Vera looked and smelled bad. Her rational thinking left her after the beating. It always appeared that Vera was looking for someone or something.

People stopped ridiculing her, and that's because no one recognized her. Whenever Vera saw a little boy, she would call him Ron. Believing it was Ron, she would tell the little boy, "Don't run. Mama won't hurt you. I won't hurt you."

One day, Vera snatched a doll from a little girl who was standing at the bus stop with her mother. Vera snatched the doll and ran into the alley. "That lady took my doll," the little girl hollered.

"That's all right," the little girl's mother said. "Let her have it. I'll get you another one."

Over the years, Vera lost her mind. She constantly held the doll closely and tightly.

On the first cold night of one winter season, Vera took her warm layer of clothing and wrapped it around the doll. A few days later, a passersby found Vera frozen to death. In her rattled mind, Vera had believed she'd been given a second chance to do right by Ron. When the passersby found the frozen woman, she was holding the doll so tightly they couldn't pry it from her arms. Vera had died believing she was protecting Ron from the cold.

No next of kin claimed the body, and no one knew who the woman was, as she had no ID on her. The city buried her.

*   *   *

Lisa graduated with honors. She became Randy's business manager. Lisa and Randy assume that Vera ran off with some man she met. Brother and sister never mentioned their mother's name among themselves again.

One day while sitting in her office, Lisa remembered something she had overheard Jackie say when Lisa was a little girl. "One day, Vera will reap what she's sow."

Without thinking, Lisa blurted out, "And sow she did."

On Baker Street